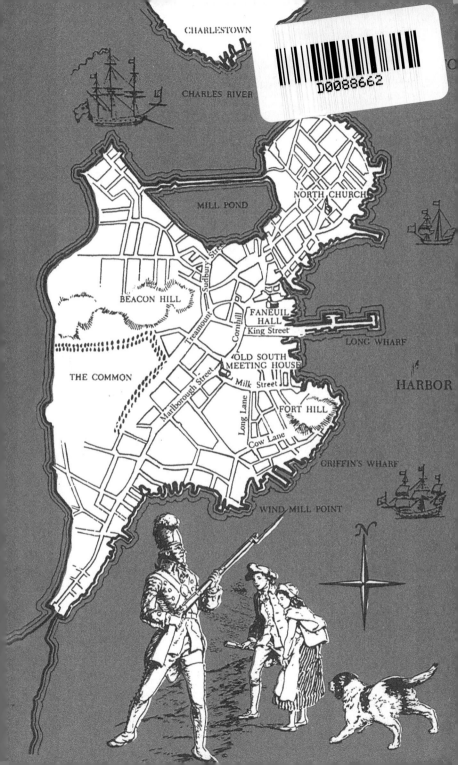

WE WERE THERE

At the Boston
Tea Party

*Three hundred and forty-two chests of tea were
dumped into the harbor that night*

WE WERE THERE
At the Boston
Tea Party

Robert N. Webb

Illustrated by
E. F. Ward

Dover Publications, Inc.
Mineola, New York

Bibliographical Note

This Dover edition, first published in 2013, is an unabridged republication of the work originally published in 1956 by Grosset & Dunlap, New York.

Library of Congress Cataloging-in-Publication Data

Webb, Robert N.
    We were there at the Boston Tea Party / Robert N. Webb; illustrated by E.F. Ward.
        p. cm.
    "This Dover edition, first published in 2013, is an unabridged republication of the work originally published in 1956 by Grosset & Dunlap, New York."
    Summary: "New England is ripe for revolution in the fall of 1773, and a brother and sister carry secret messages to Sam Adams, Paul Revere, and other patriots"—Provided by publisher.
    ISBN-13: 978-0-486-49260-5 (pbk.)
    ISBN-10: 0-486-49260-5
    [1. Boston Tea Party, Boston, Mass., 1773—Fiction. 2. Brothers and sisters—Fiction. 3. Spies—Fiction. 4. Boston (Mass.)—History—Colonial period, ca. 1600-1775—Fiction.] I. Title.

PZ7.W3836We 2013
[Fic]—dc23

2013019324

Manufactured in the United States by Courier Corporation
49260503   2015
www.doverpublications.com

For
KINK *and* JUDY

Contents

Contents

Illustrations

WE WERE THERE
At the **Boston Tea Party**

CHAPTER ONE

A Ship Is Sighted

JEREMY WINTHROP was lying flat on his back, half asleep, half awake, all comfortable. His sister Deliverance was seated about two feet back of his sandy-haired head. She plucked a dried milkweed stalk, leaned over, and brushed it across his nose.

"Stop that, Del!"

"Fine ship watcher you are," she scoffed. "Where do you expect the ship to come from—out of the sky? That's the only place you've been looking."

Jeremy grunted. "Don't bother me."

"Maybe it will come from behind that little cloud over there," she joked.

Jeremy remained silent.

"Jeremy . . . Jeremy! I think I see a ship coming!"

"Ungh," was the only answer from the dreaming Jeremy.

"Hand me Grandpa's spyglass, Jeremy."

"Get it yourself." The glass was almost touching Jeremy's hand.

"Well! Of all the lazy boys!"

There was a moment's silence as Del adjusted the long spyglass. Then she pointed it out over Boston Harbor.

"Jeremy!"

From the tone of Del's voice, Jeremy knew instantly that this time his sister was not teasing.

"Jeremy! The ship! I'm sure I see it!"

Jeremy sprang to his feet. He raced to the edge of the bluff overlooking the harbor. Del was right behind him.

"Give me the glass, Del!" He held out his hand.

Quickly adjusting the long glass to his own eyesight, Jeremy closed his left eye and aimed the glass at the oncoming ship. She was a real beauty, her great white sails bellying out from her three tall masts. The ship was rounding the harbor off Dorchester Heights, making her last tack for the portward run.

"Can you see her name yet, Jeremy?" Del asked.

Jeremy shook his head. "Not yet. Not quite. Be able to in a few minutes, though."

The boy and girl were on Wind Mill Point. From where they stood, some thirty feet above sea level, they commanded a perfect view of both the wide, sweeping harbor, and the town of Boston as well. The tall steeple of North Church could be seen sticking up like a needle above the three-story brick houses with their flat roofs and balustrades. Earlier, the children had picked out Faneuil Hall, Old South Meeting House, and other taller structures as they looked over the town. Here and there could be seen the few two-story, cement-plastered houses with their peaked roofs, which had survived the great fire of 1679.

On three sides of the town, the masts of ships at anchor swayed gently in the wind. There were so many of them, they seemed to form a long, curving line of pickets fencing the town in.

But little traffic stirred through the crooked, narrow streets. Here and there a horse-drawn cart moved slowly along.

It was a beautiful, crisp, clear morning, late in autumn, Sunday, November 28, 1773. The sky was as blue as the eyes of a china doll. A few tiny white

*The tall steeple of North Church could be seen
sticking up like a needle*

clouds, ever so high, moved lazily across the sky.

Jeremy, standing straight and strong, was nearly six feet tall, although only fourteen years old. He seemed to be leaning forward, he was so intent. Every muscle in his young body strained as he tried to make out the ship's name. The slight breeze barely stirred the lock of sandy hair that was forever dangling over his forehead. He was not what people would call a handsome boy. But his blue eyes, set wide apart, were clear, steady, alertly ready to take in the wide world about him. A few freckles, hardly noticeable, were sprayed across his nose. His mouth was large. It turned up at the corners in a shy, warm smile.

His sister Del, just one year younger, stood with a hand resting on Jeremy's shoulder. She, too, gave the impression of straining forward. Tall, though not so tall as her brother, she was his opposite in appearance in every detail. Her hair was dark, waving gently across her smooth forehead. Her eyes were nearly black, and they seemed to be flashing. A nicely shaped little nose led down to a small, flowerlike mouth, raspberry red on this chilly day. Her slender figure, now so taut with excitement, was straight.

Suddenly Jeremy strained forward even farther.

"Del! I think I can make out her name," he exclaimed. "Remember the letters as I read them off."

Del's hand clenched even harder on Jeremy's shoulder.

Her brother spoke. "Here's the first letter. It's . . . it's D. Yes . . . D. It must be the D . . . A . . . Yes the next letter's R! D-A-R-T— It is! It is! It's the *Dartmouth!*"

The *Dartmouth!* One of the three ships all Boston had been waiting for. The ship whose hated cargo had so stirred up Bostonians that angry words were heard in every inn and meeting place. On the Common, a public park where cattle once grazed, no group of men gathered without discussing the expected arrival of the tea ships.

To the people of the Massachusetts Bay Colony, the tea ships stood for tyranny, the tyranny of King George III of England. The King thought Parliament had the right to tax the colonists as it wished, and to do what it liked with the money. The colonists thought this was unfair, and began to stop buying anything from England on which they had to pay a tax. When Parliament decided to set a tax on tea, the colonists bought the cheaper, smuggled Dutch tea instead, on which, of course, there was no tax.

This made the King very angry, and he and his chief cabinet minister, Lord North, worked out a plan to force the tea tax on the colonists. The East India Company, which supplied England's tea, also had to pay a tax to the King. If the company were allowed to ship tea to the colonies without paying the tax, Lord North suggested, then they could make the price of their tea lower than the Dutch tea. The colonists would buy England's tea again, even though they still would be made to pay a tax of three pence on each pound of tea.

Lord North went before the Parliament and asked for permission to carry out this plan. Parliament granted permission and the Tea Act was passed. No one from America had anything to say as to whether or not it should be passed.

"This is taxation without representation!" thundered the colonists.

This high-handed act of Parliament caused much alarm. It was now that Americans were to determine whether they were to be free men or slaves.

Since word had been received that the tea ships

actually had sailed from England, the angrily smoldering temper of Boston burst into flames.

Jeremy and Del had attended crowded meetings of angry citizens at Faneuil Hall and Old South Meeting House. They had heard repeated time and time again the ugly words of Lord North. "Drunken ragamuffins," he had called the colonists. He had gone even further and said, "I am determined to bring America to the King's feet."

Jeremy and Del had listened solemnly as Samuel Adams, a well-known Boston patriot, addressed one of the meetings.

"This unhappy contest will end in rivers of blood," Mr. Adams said, "but America may wash her hands in innocence." He paused and then: "No one can foretell what violence the arrival of the tea ships may bring on. Yet, whatever action is taken, it should not be taken in the heat of anger. Rather we should be steadfastly guided by the knowledge that our cause is a just one and, with God's help, we will reach our goal."

The day after the meeting, Jeremy and Del had gone to Mr. Adams, whose home was right next door to the Winthrop house. They had asked him how they could help in the fight for freedom.

Mr. Adams had smiled at the two eager children. Then he had said, quite seriously, "There is a way in which you can help us greatly. Spend as much time as you can watching for the arrival of the tea ships. When you see one or all of them, let me know immediately."

So even though it was a Sunday, Jeremy and Del had been allowed to watch for the tea ships, because their arrival was of such importance to America's future. Usually, after going to early church services, the two youngsters stayed home, spending the Sabbath quietly.

And now the *Dartmouth* was here, and tea was the cargo in its hold.

Tea! A word spat from the mouth as if it were a swear word.

"It's the tea ship all right," said Jeremy.

"You're sure, Jeremy? Positive?" his sister asked.

"Indeed, yes, Del. Here, look for yourself."

Del took the long glass, raised it to her eye, and focused it on the oncoming ship.

"You're right, Jeremy. It's the *Dartmouth,* all right. How long before she'll enter the port?"

Jeremy cleared his throat. This was man's business, to answer such a question. "Well," he said, his tone almost solemn, "I calculate, with the wind on her lee freshenin' a mite, she ought to drop her hook in about three hours."

Del clapped her hand over her mouth, squealing with laughter at the seriousness of her brother's words.

"Well, now," she mimicked. "You calculate that with the wind— Oh, Jeremy, you're so funny!"

Jeremy was indignant. "Now look here, Sis—"

"You look here," she replied. "Just because Grandpa Winthrop was a sailing captain doesn't mean you know all about ships. Don't be so bigety!"

"What did you ask me for then? Crickety, Del, I was just trying to give you a good answer."

"Oh, you! Don't you know I'm just joking?"

Jeremy's good humor returned. "All right, Sis. I wasn't angry. Come on now, we've got to get the news of the ship to Mr. Adams as quickly as we can."

As the two turned to go, they stopped short. In their excitement, they hadn't seen the redcoated figure of a British soldier slip quietly up behind them. Now he was only a few feet away.

"Stay where you are," he ordered. His musket was in his hands, his thumb on the cocking piece. "What ship is that out there, making into port?"

Jeremy looked at Del. Both realized instantly that the British soldier had been sent out, as they had been, to spot the arrival of the *Dartmouth*. But without a glass, and the soldier had none, he was not able to make out the ship's name.

"Ship?" said Jeremy stupidly. "What ship is he talking 'bout, Del?"

Del shook her head. "There are lots of ships."

"Now see here, you two. You know what ship I mean. I've been watching you, both of you. I saw you jumping fit to fall off the bluff, so excited were you."

Jeremy and Del were slowly sidling away. Jeremy whispered, "Let's make a run for it."

Del nodded her head.

"Oh, no, you don't!" the Redcoat exclaimed. "You stand right there, unless you want to feel some hot lead. Now, I'll just take that glass and see for myself, I will. Hand it over."

Jeremy took a step forward, carefully extending the glass.

Oh, no! thought Del. *Don't, Jeremy! Don't! He*

"Stay where you are," he ordered

mustn't get the ship's name. Mr. Sam Adams has to know first!

Now only about three feet separated Jeremy from the Redcoat. "Lobsterback," that was what Jeremy was calling him in his mind. The name the colonists had for the soldiers of the British Army stationed in the colony was an apt one. The red swallow-tailed coat of their uniform suggested the back of a boiled lobster.

As the soldier extended his hand for the glass, Jeremy suddenly charged forward, knocking the gun to the ground, and sending the redcoat sprawling.

"Run, Del! Run!"

The boy and girl dashed down the slope. Quickly they dodged behind some trees and continued running. They twisted their way through the trees, making an impossible target, even if the Lobsterback should try to fire. Jeremy felt fairly certain he wouldn't.

In a few minutes, they stopped and looked back. They could see the soldier brushing sand off his red uniform. Then he bent to retrieve his gun. He was turning back to the harbor as Del and Jeremy burst into laughter.

"Think he'll report *that* to King George?" Jeremy asked.

Del laughed. "If Mr. Adams' dog Queue had been with us, King George would have heard that soldier's howls clear over in London!"

It took the two youngsters, racing through the woods into the narrow, winding streets of Boston, just under half an hour to reach the home of Sam Adams on Purchase Street. As they passed their own house, they waved to their mother, who was standing on the steps. Then, instead of boiling into the Adams home, they slowed their pace to a sedate walk. One didn't burst in on Mr. Sam Adams.

Mistress Adams answered their knock.

"Do come in, Deliverance and Jeremy."

The boy and girl bowed politely, acknowledging the friendly invitation.

"We should like to see Mr. Adams, Mistress Adams, if we may," Jeremy said.

"We wouldn't disturb him," Del cut in, "but he told us—"

"Not at all. Not at all, children. I believe Mr. Adams is expecting you. He's in his study. Come in."

She led them through the sparsely, even poorly, furnished living room. Sam Adams, though a leader in the town of Boston, indeed, a leader throughout Massachusetts, was not a wealthy man. Only Mistress Adams' careful shopping, her stretching of every penny, kept the Adams family going. In the ways of business, Mr. Adams never could seem to make a success. But as a leader of men, as a man dedicated to the service of his country, no man was greater, not even John Hancock or Josiah Quincy or Paul Revere.

Mistress Adams knocked gently on the door of the study.

"Yes? Please enter."

The door swung open. Mr. Adams was seated, writing. He lifted a quill pen from a page of foolscap, sanded his writing carefully to dry the ink, and placed his pen precisely in a narrow tray.

"Ah. The Winthrop children, Deliverance and Jeremy. Please find chairs, and seat yourselves."

Mr. Adams rose slowly from his Windsor writing chair with its one large, flat-surfaced arm, and placed the foolscap on his desk. His body was frail. He was slightly stooped. His hands shook endlessly. He was not an old man, just fifty-one, yet a sickness years before had left his body little more than a shell. But if his body was frail, his mind was strong and his heart big. There was greatness in the calm serenity of his face. His eyes were clear and challenging.

The boy and girl still stood. It was not for them to be seated when Mr. Sam Adams stood. Even though their hearts were beating quickly with the excitement of their escape from the Lobsterback and the importance of their news, they curbed themselves. Mr. Sam Adams was a man who commanded respect without ever demanding it. People were anxious to hear his spoken words. People waited for Mr. Sam Adams to speak first.

"And now, I believe, no doubt, you have brought me some word?"

Del looked at Jeremy. She wanted him to be the spokesman.

"Yes, sir, Mr. Adams," Jeremy said.

"Please be seated."

Jeremy and Del watched the man lower himself into his chair, then seated themselves.

"Yes?" There was a slight, questioning smile on Mr. Adams' strong face.

"The ship, sir. The *Dartmouth*. We spotted her

rounding Dorchester Heights. She should stand off Griffin's Wharf within three hours."

Mr. Adams nodded his head. He leaned back in his chair, closed his eyes momentarily, in deep thought.

"So, the *Dartmouth* is here. Come at last. Only the *Dartmouth?* There were no other ships?"

"Not within our sight, sir. They may be right behind the *Dartmouth*. But we thought you would want to know immediately."

"True. True. Please accept my thanks, my most sincere thanks . . . The time for action is now upon us."

Again he closed his eyes. The boy and girl waited quietly for their dismissal.

Mr. Adams spoke again. "The *Dartmouth* is here, bearing in her hold the brew that may steep us in a war of revolution."

"Sir?"

Del and Jeremy looked at one another. What did he mean?

But they were not to learn just then. Quickly Mr. Adams straightened up. He had said it was now the time for action, and he was prepared to take steps at once.

"There are messages that must be sent out. If you two will now excuse me, I must to work."

The boy and girl stood.

"Yes, sir. And sir . . . ?" Jeremy said.

Mr. Adams looked up. "Yes?"

"Mr. Adams," Jeremy asked, "is there any news of Queue?"

A quick frown passed over Mr. Adams' face.

"No, I fear not. And how I miss him! An ugly dog, perhaps. But a thinking one, as many a Lobsterback can tell you."

"We hope he's found soon."

"Found?" Mr. Adams repeated. "He's found, all right. He's been found by the British soldiers, and they're keeping him prisoner, just to rile up 'the rebel Adams,' as they call me."

Jeremy looked at Del, and at once they both knew what they were going to do next. Even if it meant risking their necks to slip into the British encampment, they were going to do just that, and get Queue back.

CHAPTER TWO

Queue Goes to Dinner

It was just about noon when Jeremy and Del left Sam Adams' house. They had calmed down considerably from the excitement of their morning adventure. Both were thinking of the great Newfoundland dog, held captive by the British soldiers. It was one thing to decide to enter the British soldiers' camp and free Queue. It was quite another, though, to carry out the deed. It would be a dangerous mission. And while neither Jeremy nor Del was afraid, both were sensible enough to know the risk they would be taking.

"Jeremy," Del spoke softly as the two walked slowly toward their own house, "shall we go over to the British camp right away?"

"I don't know, Del. I haven't made any plans. Have you any ideas?" he inquired.

"Well, we'd better go home first. There may be

something Mother wants us to do. We've been gone all morning."

"It's dinnertime, too. Are you hungry?"

"Not very. But we'd better eat, or Mother and Father will suspect we're up to something."

"Yes. But let's hurry. I think this will be a good time to get into the camp. The soldiers will be eating soon. My guess is they'll never think anyone would try to take Queue in broad daylight."

The children's dinner that noon was roast venison, from a deer that Jeremy himself had shot only two weeks before. He had gone hunting with Mr. Sam Adams' son, with Queue along, of course. The bright red cranberries, now steaming hot and smelling so good, had been gathered by Del. Jeremy and Del had thought they weren't hungry, but they quickly demolished a whole loaf of their mother's homemade bread.

Between mouthfuls of food, they told their parents of the arrival of the *Dartmouth,* but they were careful not to say that Queue was missing.

"I dread the thought of what the arrival of that ship can mean," Giles Winthrop, their father, said.

"Mr. Adams said that now will be the time for action," Del said.

"Yes," Jeremy cut in, "and he said the *Dartmouth* bears the brew that may steep us in revolution. What did he mean, Father?"

Mr. Winthrop shook his head. "A wise man, Mr. Adams, but there are too many hotheads amongst us. These are dangerous times. You ask what Mr. Adams meant, son?" Mr. Winthrop thought for a minute. "I fear he is thinking of war. That's where this cargo of taxed tea may lead us all. And war, son, no matter how just we may think the cause, is a horrible state. Wars settle little, as someday we may learn. But let us hope that there may yet be found some other solution than armed force."

Mr. Winthrop arose. "If you will excuse me," he said to Mistress Winthrop, "I'll return to my study."

The children watched their father leave the room. He was a professor at Harvard College, and when at home, spent much of his time among his books and papers. He also taught Jeremy and Del their lessons. While this meant they did not have to go to a regular school, secretly they thought their father made them work even harder.

Jeremy looked at Del. Both loved their father and admired him. But he was such a quiet man.

Not like Mr. Sam Adams, or Paul Revere, or John Hancock. *They* held meetings and made plans. Jeremy often wished his father would show more interest in the cause of freedom which now had all of Boston, all of Massachusetts Bay Colony, so ready for desperate action. And lately, from things Mr. Winthrop said, Jeremy sometimes wondered if perhaps his father wasn't even favoring the British cause. Such thoughts Jeremy always quickly put aside. He did not want to believe them.

"Anything we must do this afternoon, Mother?" he asked now.

"No. Jeremy. If your lessons are finished, you and Del may go out. It's such a lovely day, and we won't be having many more. Run along, both of you."

"I'll help you with the dishes," Del offered.

"No. You may draw the water when you return, and do them tonight."

"Thank you, Mother." Del walked around the table and threw her arms around her mother.

"Come on, Del. Let's be off," Jeremy urged. But he too paused long enough to give his mother a quick hug.

"The bread was wonderful, Mother," he said.

Jeremy and Del walked quickly along Sudbury Street until they reached the point where it became Treamount. At School Street they halted.

"Any plans?" Del asked.

"I'm thinking. Don't bother me," Jeremy mumbled.

"Very well, Mister Brains." She stressed the word "Mister." "But see if you can think faster than you usually do. Queue could die of old age if we wait for you to think up some involved plan. Why don't we just go in and take him?"

Jeremy glared at his sister.

They were sauntering along now, headed for the Common. Opposite the Old Granary Burying Place which was on one corner of the Common, the two halted again. Jeremy was looking into the graveyard.

In it, a simple headstone marked the site where

his best friend lay buried. On the headstone was the legend:

CHRISTOPHER SNYDER
Born Jan. 5, 1759
Died Feb. 22, 1770

Poor Chris, Jeremy thought. How many happy times had he and Del had with Chris! They still saw Chris's father from time to time. He was a German baker, and oh, how many hot buns and jelly crumpets fresh from the oven had they eaten when Chris was alive!

Jeremy and Del remembered with a shudder the

day Chris was killed, three years ago. Chris had been just Jeremy's age. The three had been playing together that very morning. They had separated, to go home to dinner. Chris, on his way home, had stopped where a crowd had gathered and was hurling insults at a trader who had earned the town's hatred by insisting on selling tea. Suddenly, in the heat of the catcalls, the noise, the angry motion of the crowd, someone had fired a shot to break up the gathering. The shot had struck poor Chris, killing him instantly.

All the Sons of Liberty attended the lad's funeral. Five hundred children, led by Del and Jeremy, walked in couples in front of his bier.

Nearly fifteen hundred citizens followed, on foot and in chaises and chariots.

Many fine, strong people were to give up their lives in the Revolutionary War for America's freedom. Eleven-year-old Christopher Snyder—Jeremy and Del's best friend—was the first to lose his life in the great battle for independence. Strangely enough, Christopher Snyder died on February 22, 1770, the thirty-eighth birthday of another Son of Liberty—George Washington.

"Are you thinking about Chris?" Del asked.

"Yes, Del," Jeremy answered.

"So was I," she sighed.

Jeremy remembered, too, that it was here, in Old Granary, that he and Del had first met Hubert Stubbs, a sergeant of the British Guard. They had come to put spring flowers on Chris's grave. On arriving, they had seen—of all things—a Redcoat kneeling at their friend's grave! They had charged up to him angrily, only to find that he too was placing a basket of mayflowers on the mound. Ashamed, they waited quietly while the sergeant said his brief prayer. Later, in talking to the hearty Stubbs, they learned the sergeant had a young brother back in London about the same age as

Chris. The lonely soldier and the boy had often talked and joked together. With this bond between them, Jeremy and Del had become close, but secret, friends of Sergeant Stubbs. Even old Redcoat-hating Queue had given in a little. He just growled half-heartedly when the good sergeant came in view.

CHRISTOPHER SNYDER

BORN   JAN. 5, 1759
DIED   FEB. 22, 1770

Jeremy thought about Sergeant Stubbs now. It gave him an idea.

"Del!" he said excitedly. "Do you think Sergeant Stubbs would help us get Queue back?"

"Stubbsy? I don't know. He might."

"Let's find him, and ask him."

"But Jeremy, suppose he won't," Del objected. "Suppose we tell him what we want to do, and then he won't help. He could tell the other guards to be on the watch."

"Oh, I don't think he would do that. Queue never bit him."

"Well, all right then," Del answered doubtfully.

The two walked across the Common toward the few tents where the Guard lived. Most of the British soldiers were billeted in the homes of Boston families, but the Guard stayed on the Common. The Guard wasn't large, and many of the British soldiers had been allowed to take jobs to add to the small pay they received from the King.

"Sergeant Stubbs is on duty this week," Jeremy said.

They found the sergeant just as he was on his way to the mess tent to join the other soldiers in their noonday meal.

"Well now," Sergeant Stubbs said. "And what would you two be up to? Heard tell that a couple of youngsters had a run-in with one of my guards this morning. Up Wind Mill Point way. Upset his dignity, it did. Couldn't 'a' been you two, could it?"

Jeremy and Del just grinned.

"And you're up to something now, I can tell. Can't fool Stubbs."

Jeremy looked at Del. Del, observing that the sergeant seemed to be in a very jolly mood, nodded her head.

"We were just wondering if we could see Queue," Jeremy said carefully.

"Queue? And why might you be a-thinkin' that ornery dog of Mr. Adams is here?"

Before they could answer they heard a series of loud barks. Queue was there, all right. He had scented his friends, and was calling for help.

"Now lookee here, you two. You wouldn't be thinkin' of letting Queue go loose, would you? Not after he all but took the breeches off two of the guards who caught him?"

Jeremy and Del nodded their heads.

"Thought as much. Now I'm Sergeant of the Guard here, and bein' such, it's my duty to King George himself to see that nothing's taken from our camp. I don't rightly hold though, with kidnaping a man's dog. No, sir. That I don't. Not even Mr. Adams' mutt."

Hope spread over the faces of the boy and girl.

"Nevertheless, I feel it my soldier's duty not to tell anyone that Queue's tied up to the third tent behind the mess tent. And I wouldn't be a-sayin' that since all my guards is eatin', there ain't none a-watchin' him now. No, sir. I wouldn't be doin' my duty if I said such things out loud. Not in front of two conspirators."

Jeremy and Del grinned.

"Good thing there's no boy around here with a sharp knife. For Queue's tied with a right stout piece of rope. And it's a good thing that no young slip of a girl is around here to stand lookout if any of the guards was to leave the mess tent right soon. No. All's well, as the saying goes. And here goes Sergeant Stubbs to fill his belly."

They watched the sergeant disappear into the mess tent. Then, quickly, Jeremy and Del raced to the group of tents. Del stood just behind the mess tent, keeping a sharp lookout for Lobsterbacks while Jeremy crept quietly back to the third tent. There, sure enough, was Queue. He was tied to a tent pole.

As Jeremy approached, the huge Newfoundland dog leaped up, his front paws reaching Jeremy's shoulders, his long, red tongue trying to lick Jeremy's face. Queue was a large dog, weighing nearly a hundred and fifty pounds. He had long, shaggy hair. Floppy ears hung far down his big head. A blunt nose gave a comical expression to his intelligent face.

"Down, boy, down!" Jeremy bade him. "Quiet, Queue!"

Quickly Jeremy pulled out his knife and slashed at the rope holding the dog. Freed, the dog strained to race about, but Jeremy held his collar. The boy bent down and whispered into one floppy ear, "Home, Queue. Home."

Queue cocked his head inquiringly. He seemed to be thinking over the command Jeremy had just given him. Then, apparently, Queue decided he had something else to do before obeying.

He pulled loose from Jeremy, turned and darted toward the mess tent where Del was standing guard. He stopped briefly to lick a quick welcome on Del, then whirled and dashed straight into the mess tent.

In it, some thirty members of the Guard were seated on either side of a long, narrow table. Without pausing, Queue leaped. He wasn't going home

without paying these Redcoats back for holding him prisoner. Bounding on the table, he raced from one end to another, upsetting steaming soup bowls, knocking joints of meat helter-skelter. Plates, knives, and forks were sent slithering onto the floor. The clatter of crockery mingled with the soldiers' shouting and cursing. Yelps of pain echoed Queue's barking as scalding chowder poured in the laps of indignant soldiers. In spite of an artillery fire of bread, spoons, and plates, Queue raced back and forth. Only a well-aimed soup bowl on his rump warned the dog to leave while victory was his.

Dashing out of the tent, Queue almost bowled Jeremy and Del over. His deed for the cause of liberty was accomplished. He decided his two chums could take care of themselves, and now he was off for home.

"There they are! There they are!" shouted one of the guards. "The same two rascals who knocked me over this morning. They did this. Grab 'em!"

It was the very same soldier Jeremy and Del had encountered that morning.

The boy and girl fled, running at top speed. A shot rang out, and Jeremy heard the angry hiss of a bullet by his head. Then they were out of range, and headed for home.

In the front of Mr. Adams' house the boy and girl paused. "Did you ever see anything funnier?" Del laughed.

Jeremy was doubled up, gasping for breath from the frenzied run, and trying to hold his laughter in.

Then they heard Mr. Adams' voice. He had come to the front door. Queue was beside him. Mr. Adams was stroking the dog's head.

"I imagine I have you two to thank for the return of my dog."

Jeremy and Del nodded their heads.

"My most heartfelt thanks to you both. I am so happy to have my dog back that I shan't scold you. But it was a foolish, yea, even a dangerous thing to do."

The boy and girl looked guiltily at one another.

"Nothing like that must happen again . . ." Mr. Adams paused, then added, "But I admire your spirit!"

Big grins now spread over the faces of the brother and sister.

"We won't do anything like that any more, Mr. Adams," Jeremy promised.

"No. I'm sure you won't," Mr. Adams said with a smile. "Unless . . . unless Queue turns up missing again."

Then his face became deadly serious. "Could you two step into my study for a moment?"

"Yes, sir." They spoke as one.

As they entered the study, they saw that Mr.

Adams had not been alone. Seated were Mr. Josiah Quincy and Dr. Joseph Warren, two other patriotic leaders.

"I believe you have met the Winthrop children, have you not, gentlemen?"

The men bowed gravely.

"The arrival of the tea ship *Dartmouth,*" Mr. Adams said, addressing Jeremy and Del, "has set in motion events which will chart the future of our nation. None of us can foretell what that future will hold. But we have decided on a course, and we have dedicated our lives to it."

He paused, and cleared his throat.

"It is of the greatest urgency that Mr. John Hancock be found and given this document which I hold in my hand."

Again Mr. Adams paused, and looked at the children.

"It would not be wise, at this time, for any of us to be seen approaching Mr. Hancock. Already there is much suspicion on the part of Governor Hutchinson and his Redcoat spies that something is afoot. Therefore, after consulting with Mr. Quincy and Dr. Warren, I have decided to ask you, Jeremy and Del, if you could work with us—if you could become our messengers. Messengers of Liberty, I believe we could call you."

Suddenly the hearts of the boy and girl were beating rapidly.

Mr. Adams continued, "You have already proven that you are the match of the Lobsterbacks. Nay, more than that, you have bested them twice in a single day.

"Were this note I hold to fall into British hands, I am certain that our plans for this evening would be upset with startling speed. We sorely need two wily couriers to carry it swiftly to Mr. Hancock. Do you two care to run the risk of delivering this message?"

Too excited to speak, Jeremy and Del could only nod their heads.

"And not get caught? By now, you probably are somewhat under suspicion yourselves."

Del could hold herself in no longer.

"Mr. Adams, I have an idea. Let us take Queue along just as though we were taking him for a walk. The British, we know, have had enough of Queue for one day. We'll frolic with him as though 'twere all in fun—let him fetch sticks and all."

"A capital idea," Josiah Quincy said. "The lass

is quick-witted. She would use the dog to throw off suspicion. Do you agree, Joseph?"

Dr. Warren nodded. Del, blushing, curtsied prettily, her head spinning at the compliment.

"Then here you are, Jeremy," Mr. Adams said.

He handed Jeremy the note, leaned forward and said, "You'll find Mr. Hancock, I believe, at the Blue Lantern Tavern."

Jeremy and Del slipped out of the house, into the darkening twilight.

CHAPTER THREE

Caught by the British

A BRISK northeast wind had sprung up, bringing with it the promise of snow. Jeremy and Del buttoned the collars of their cloaks more tightly around their throats. The days had grown shorter, and full night was nearly upon them, although it was not quite five o'clock. Queue whined, impatient to be off.

"We'll have to hurry, Jeremy," Del said.

"Yes, I know. We must be back in time for supper."

"And before Father misses us. Jeremy—" Del paused. "Jeremy, what about Father? Doesn't he feel the same as Mr. Adams does about the tea tax?"

They walked along nearly half a block before Jeremy answered.

"I don't know, Del. Sometimes I wonder. He

hasn't been to any of the meetings at Faneuil Hall or Old South, either."

"He and Mr. Adams used to be such good friends," Del said, "but I haven't seen them together lately."

There was a heavy frown now on Jeremy's usually smiling face.

"You don't think," Del continued, "that he's a Tory—that he's on the side of the King?"

"Don't say it!" Jeremy cut in sharply. But he, too, was worried. The doubts which he tried to keep out of his mind came back often these days.

The youngsters had reached the corner of Marlborough and Milk streets. Across from them stood the Old South Meeting House. Del and Jeremy drew back quickly into the shadow of a doorway as they spotted the Redcoat guard in front of the building.

"If Stubbs is in command of the Guard," Jeremy whispered to Del, "we're safe. But if it's Lieutenant Snipe, then we'll have to backtrack and take the long way around through Summer Street and Cow Lane. I'm going to slip up closer and see. You stay here. Keep Queue with you."

Lieutenant Snipe was one of the most hated of

all the officers of the British Guard. He had come from England three years before, just after the removal of British Captain Thomas Preston. From the very first day of his arrival, his swagger, his vanity, and his uncalled-for taunting of the citizens had earned him the name of "Snipe the Sneerer."

Snipe often boasted of what *he* would have done, had *he* been in charge of the Guard instead of Preston on that tragic day Bostonians would long remember.

"Preston was a weakling," Snipe often sneered. "Give me the same situation. I'll show these rabble turncoats how a crowd should be handled."

Three years before, a group of boys had been teasing a sentinel stationed on King Street. Captain Preston, sword in hand, had led a squad of twelve soldiers to the sentinel's rescue. By the time the squad reached King Street, a large crowd had gathered.

"Load and prime!" Preston had ordered.

A bookseller named Henry Knox rushed up to the captain.

"You're not going to fire?" Knox protested.

"I know what I'm about," Preston replied shortly.

Above the noise of the crowd, the word, "Fire!" was heard. Guns roared. Three persons were killed and eight wounded. As the wounded lay groaning, one of the soldiers deliberately aimed at a boy who was running to get clear of the crowd.

The people called this tragedy the "Boston Massacre." It took place only a short time after Chris Snyder had been killed.

It was never proven that a formal order to fire had been given. Captain Preston and the twelve soldiers were indicted for the shooting. The captain was acquitted, but the irate citizens of Boston demanded his return to England.

Bostonians would never forget the sad day of the "Massacre." Snipe's strident reminders kept the day even fresher in their minds. He talked so much about it that many came to believe he actually took part in it.

Del peeped out around the doorway. What was keeping Jeremy? Queue, who had been growling at the sight of the Redcoats, suddenly dashed off. The girl drew back into the shallow hiding place and flattened herself against the wall.

The Guard in front of Old South was being changed. It had been stationed there only recently because more and more meetings, with more and more angry citizens attending, were being held in Old South.

There had been a meeting at Old South just the night before. It had been called by Sam Adams and his Committee of Correspondence. It was this committee which kept the other colonies informed about the action Massachusetts Bay was taking in the long struggle against the acts of Parliament and the King.

Neither Jeremy nor Del had attended this meeting. They knew, though, that it had been called because the tea ships were expected any day. They had both read about the meeting in the *Boston Post-Boy,* one of the town's newspapers.

"Adams," the article in the newspaper had stated, "drew up to his full height; and, while his frame trembled at the energy of his soul, he stretched forth his hand as if upheld by the strength of thousands and said: 'When our liberty is gone, history and experience will teach us that an increase in inhabitants is but an increase in slaves.' "

In the other newspapers, the *Boston News-Letter* and the *Boston Gazette,* articles declared that

"Whoever should purchase and use this tea would drink political damnation to themselves."

Del, crouching in the doorway where Jeremy had told her to stay, was becoming impatient. "Hurry, Jeremy, hurry!" she whispered to herself. Feminine curiosity overcame her. She stepped out of the doorway. Her eyes strained as she peered through the darkness, hoping to see Jeremy's shadowy figure appear.

Suddenly she felt a heavy hand grasp her roughly by the shoulder. Her startled scream was cut short as the Redcoat's other hand was clapped tightly over her mouth.

Moving swiftly but silently, after he left Del, Jeremy took advantage of the darkness to slip around behind Old South. He knew the building well and was soon at a small door in the rear. Cautiously he pulled the door open, then stood silently for a moment to catch any sound that would tell him someone else was in the building.

Hearing nothing, he carefully moved toward the front of the building. He crouched low, feeling his way along the stall-shaped family pews. These pews were waist high, each one long enough to seat a family of eight or ten. Jeremy was completely hidden by the pews, save now and then when he would raise his head above their sides, and peer intently about, to make sure he was not spotted if anyone else was in the room. He wanted to get to a window near the main entrance which fronted on Marlborough Street, later called Washington Street.

The stillness and the darkness seemed to press in on Jeremy as if trying to hold him back. He slowly raised his head. Carefully, his eyes now accustomed to the darkness, he looked around. He could just see the outlines of the double balconies which extended around three sides of the huge room. Jeremy was directly in front of the fifteen-foot high pulpit from which the stirring orations of Adams, Hancock, and other patriots were delivered.

Suddenly his heart started pounding violently. He crouched even lower so that his body would be completely hidden by one of the pews. Someone else was in the room. He could tell it. He could feel it. He remained perfectly motionless. His body was rigid. Every muscle was tense, ready for action.

Then Jeremy let out a long sigh of relief as he

felt Queue's cold nose press against his hand. He had forgotten to close the rear door, and Queue had trailed him into the building.

Feeling much relieved—although he wouldn't admit even to himself that he had been scared—Jeremy stole silently toward the window. It felt good to have Queue by his side. It was rather spooky all alone there in the dark.

Slowly Jeremy raised his head until his eyes were just above the window sill. He had a fine view. One of the guards was holding a torchlight. Jeremy spotted Sergeant Stubbs instantly. And then, to his disgust, he also saw Lieutenant Snipe.

Well, that was that. It was only a short block from Old South to the Blue Lantern Tavern, where John Hancock was waiting. But to get there, Jeremy and Del would have to pass right by the Guard. They would have to go back the way they'd come, and take the long way around. It would be precious time wasted, but there was nothing else to do.

A low growl came from Queue. Jeremy placed his hand on the dog's back to quiet him, and felt the dog's hackles rise.

"What is it, Queue?"

Then Jeremy saw. The Guard had suddenly moved off at a stiff trot toward the corner where he had left Del!

Jeremy threw open the front door of Old South and dashed into the street. Queue shot passed him at full speed after the Redcoats.

Then Jeremy heard Del's voice.

"Jeremy! Jeremy!" she called out. "Run! Run! They've caught me."

In a split second Jeremy made his decision. He knew it was of great importance to deliver the message to John Hancock, but the safety of his sister must come first.

As fast as he could run, Jeremy tore across the street headed toward the Lobsterbacks surrounding Del.

Queue was racing around the group of soldiers, snapping at their heels, adding his barks and growls to the general commotion.

Jeremy burst through the circle of guards and rushed up to Del.

"Are you all right, Del? They didn't hurt you, did they?"

Del, trying bravely to hold back her tears, shook her head.

"No. I'm all right. But Jeremy . . . what about the . . ."

Jeremy moved quickly to his sister's side, and put his arm around her shoulder, as if to comfort her. With lips pressed close to her ear, he whispered rapidly, "Don't worry. I'm going to get you out of this. Get the message to Mr. Hancock."

His back to the group of soldiers, Jeremy quickly took Mr. Adams' note from his pocket, and slipped it beneath Del's cloak.

"Here now, what's going on there?" Lieutenant Snipe demanded, stepping up to the two youngsters.

Jeremy swung around. "What do you mean by holding my sister?" he demanded bravely.

"Now, not so fast, young man," Snipe replied. "My man here," he pointed to one of the soldiers, "caught her hiding in this doorway, spying on us."

"That's right, sir." A guard stepped forward. "And they're the two what was in our camp at noontime. They're up to something."

"All right, Hammond," Lieutenant Snipe said to the soldier. "I'll find out what it is. He turned to Sergeant Stubbs. "Sergeant, take over the Guard. I'll take these two young rebels with me. When you've posted the Guard, join me in the squad room at the Castle. We'll find out what these two are up to, and we'll show them they can't go around interfering with the duties of the King's Army."

Sergeant Stubbs called the Guard to attention, then marched them off.

"All right, you two," Snipe commanded. "You'll come with me. No tricks now. You, boy," he said to Jeremy. "You walk ahead. Only one pace, though. I'm right behind you, and my hand's on my sword."

They started off. Del was at the lieutenant's side,

Jeremy just a step ahead. Jeremy's mind was in a spin. He just couldn't let Snipe take them to the Castle. The Castle, located on an island in Boston Harbor, was where the main body of the British garrison was quartered. If Snipe succeeded in getting him and Del out there, there was no telling when they might be released. Probably not until morning. And Mr. Hancock would not receive the message!

Mr. Sam Adams had trusted them! Trusted them not to be caught!

The beginnings of an idea were building up in Jeremy's mind. What was it Stubbs had said to him, just the other day? Something about Lieutenant Snipe. But what was it? Now it came to him. Stubbs had warned him and Del to be careful of Snipe. Stubbs had said, "Mighty mean he is these days, that Snipe. His feet is killin' him. Corns, you know, from his tight boots. Proud he is of his small feet. But they ain't as small as he thinks they is. Yep, his corns is actin' up again."

That was it! Cautiously Jeremy glanced over his shoulder. Then, quickly, he stopped, stepped backward and brought his foot down hard on one of Snipe's polished boots.

"Crikey!" yelled Lieutenant Snipe. He doubled over, grabbed the injured foot, and hopped around on the other.

"Now, Del! Now!" Jeremy shouted. "Run for it. I'll hold him here till you get away!"

Del wasted no time. She sped up the street, rounded a corner and was out of sight.

Jeremy turned his attention to Snipe again. Once more he tramped on a Snipe boot, the other one this time. As Lieutenant Snipe's howls of pain split the air, Jeremy knocked him over with a powerful shove. Then he turned and set off after Del.

Jeremy nearly bumped into Del as he sped around the corner.

"Hurry!" he gasped. "We must get away! And quickly!"

Even as Jeremy spoke, he and Del could hear Lieutenant Snipe calling for help.

"Turn out the Guard!" Snipe was shouting. "Stubbs! Stubbs! This way. After them!"

Del and Jeremy were worried. Both knew that bowling over a member of the Guard might be overlooked, but to attack one of the King's officers, the officer in charge of the Guard, that was a different matter.

Lieutenant Snipe wouldn't forget it. Not for a moment. Jeremy and Del would have to be extra careful now.

CHAPTER FOUR

Message Delivered

JEREMY and Del, running swiftly, reached the corner of Summer Street and Cow Lane. They halted to catch their breath. Queue, who had loped along beside them, sat on his haunches, and cocked his head at them, as if asking, "Well, what now?"

No longer could they hear Lieutenant Snipe's cries for action. They knew, though, that this didn't mean they were safe. The lieutenant was a determined man. His pride had been bruised as well as his corns. He would be out for revenge. Jeremy and Del knew that as soon as Snipe could assemble a squad of guards, he would order them to search every lane, alley, and crooked street in the area.

"This has turned out to be quite a frolic, hasn't it, Jeremy?" Del said.

"What do you mean?"

"Remember how I told Mr. Adams that we'd take Queue along, as if just out for a frolic with him? To throw off suspicion?"

Jeremy smiled and put his hand on his sister's shoulder. "Don't fret, Del. But we must make haste. It won't take Snipe very long to assemble a squad of guards. And we're honor-bound to deliver this message to Mr. Hancock. Then we must hurry home. We'll not be safe until we're there."

It was totally dark now, although not six o'clock yet. The northeast wind had brought in snow clouds.

A low growl from Queue warned the youngsters of someone's approach. From near the corner of Summer Street they could hear the loud talking of two men.

"Lobsterbacks!" Del whispered.

" 'Fraid so," Jeremy answered. "Here's what we'll do. I'll cross the street and walk along that side. They'll be looking for us together. You come along this side. I don't think they will suspect us if we're separated. Now just walk, fast, to be sure, but don't run. Maybe they won't get suspicious. Let's keep in sight of one another, though."

Jeremy crossed the cobblestone street. Del waited for Jeremy to get about twenty feet ahead. Then she started off. Queue's rising growls by her side made her feel certain that the two men just rounding the corner into Cow Lane were Redcoats.

Jeremy's plan was working out well. Walking rapidly, but not fast enough to cause notice, they turned up Long Lane until they reached Milk Street. Once again they were within a short distance of Old South, where the Redcoat Guard was on patrol.

A low whistle from Jeremy caught Del's ear. She stopped and waited until her brother crossed the street and joined her.

"If we get any nearer Old South," Jeremy said, "the Redcoats are sure to spot us. We'll cut through this lane to Water Street, then make a dash for it. The Blue Lantern's at the corner of Cornhill—just half a block."

No one had interfered with their progress. The two Redcoats who had been behind them apparently had turned up some other street. They were nowhere in sight now.

"We're all right now, Del." They could see

the Blue Lantern Tavern, only fifty yards away.

But they weren't all right. At that distance from the tavern they failed to spot a British guard standing by the door. The guard had seen John Hancock enter the tavern and had decided he'd better keep an eye on him.

If Jeremy and Del had dashed for the tavern, as planned, they would have run right into the arms of the soldier. Luck was with them, though.

All of a sudden, Queue, scenting the near-by presence of Redcoats, leaped away. He raced by the tavern, turned left toward Old South, and set upon the Guard. The soldier in front of the tavern left his post, chasing after Queue.

Jeremy looked at Del and grinned. They walked slowly to the tavern, and entered.

Was it luck? Or had Queue decided he'd have to take a hand in things to keep the youngsters safe? People said Queue was a highly intelligent dog. They said he knew exactly what he should do as Sam Adams' dog. He hated the British uniform. He had been cut and shot in several places by British soldiers because of the sharp attacks he had made on them.

Luck or not, Jeremy and Del never would have

reached the Blue Lantern Tavern safely if it hadn't been for Queue.

The Blue Lantern Tavern was a favorite place for the patriots to gather and plot their moves. A two-story brick building with a pitch roof, it stood facing Cornhill Street. An iron rod stuck out over the entrance, and from it hung a lantern. The glass of the lantern was stained blue, and the faint light it cast was the same color. It was from this lantern that the tavern took its name. The ground floor was divided into a small office, a kitchen in the rear, and one large room all the way across the front. Huge, hand-hewn beams supported the low ceiling. Wood carvings of fruit baskets and the coat of arms of Massachusetts hung on the walls.

Two-armed candlestands were placed about the

room to add to the light given off by the candle lanterns hanging on the walls.

One long table, large enough to seat thirty people, occupied the center of the room. Smaller tables, with fanback chairs, stood along the sides of the room. A roaring fire from a huge fireplace was the room's only source of heat.

As Jeremy and Del entered, their eyes searched the candlelighted room for Mr. Hancock. They spotted him having supper with Mr. Paul Revere, the silversmith.

In their clothing and their appearance, the two men were quite different. Hancock, a wealthy merchant, who at times was firmly against Mr. Adams' ideas, was a fancy dresser. This night he sat at the table dressed in gold lace and fine ruffles. At home—so it was said—he usually wore a red velvet cap over one made of fine linen. The linen of the second cap turned up three inches over the velvet one. His favorite lounging robe was a blue damask gown lined with silk. He wore white silk stockings and red morocco slippers.

Paul Revere was a plainly dressed man, not given to the finery that Hancock always wore. Revere was a true artisan who made beautiful pitchers, bowls, and plates. Often Jeremy and Del would stop in his small shop and watch him work.

Neither Jeremy nor Del knew Mr. Hancock very well. They were somewhat hesitant in approaching him. Both were glad that Paul Revere was there. He was a good friend. They spoke to him first.

"Do you two young people know Mr. Hancock?" Revere asked.

"Yes, Mr. Revere," Del replied. "Father has introduced us."

"These are Giles Winthrop's children, Mr. Hancock," Revere said to Hancock.

"Of course, of course," said John Hancock heartily. "I remember them well."

"It's you we came to see, Mr. Hancock," Jeremy said.

"Indeed? And what is it about?"

"We have a message for you—from Mr. Adams," Del said.

Jeremy handed the note to John Hancock. A frown came over Hancock's face as he read the message.

"Tonight," he said. "Adams is wasting no time. He's called a meeting at the Long Room, Paul. Of the Correspondence Committee. He'll want you, too. As for me—" Hancock paused, and turned to the children. "You're returning to Mr. Adams' house?" he inquired.

Jeremy and Del nodded their heads.

"Then tell him I shall try to be there to put my signature to his plan."

"What was all the excitement as you two came in?" Revere asked.

"Queue was chasing some Redcoats," Del answered, trying not to giggle.

"Good thing he was, too," Jeremy cut in. "Or they would have stopped us."

Jeremy didn't notice the glance Paul Revere gave to John Hancock. There was a worried frown on the silversmith's face. Always considerate of others, Revere feared for the youngsters' safety. He decided he would walk home with them.

"Mr. Hancock," Revere said, "if you will excuse me, I think I'll go over to Mr. Adams' house now. May I walk along with you two?" he asked Jeremy and Del.

"Oh, yes, Mr. Revere," Del replied.

Jeremy was glad, too. Getting back to Mr. Adams' house would have been another problem. Lieutenant Snipe and his guards would still be out searching for them. But with Paul Revere along, it wasn't likely that the Redcoats would interfere with them.

The walk back to Mr. Adams' house was without any trouble, just as Jeremy had believed. Twice, the three met British soldiers. The soldiers didn't try to stop them, though.

Again Mr. Adams was in his study. Mr. Quincy was still there.

"You found Mr. Hancock?" Mr. Adams asked.

"Yes, sir," said Jeremy. "He said he would try to come to the meeting."

"And he said he would come to put his signature to your plan," Del added hurriedly.

Josiah Quincy laughed. "That's John, all right," he said. "He's mighty proud of his signature."

Mr. Adams chuckled, then spoke to Paul Revere.

"I'm glad you came along with the children, Paul. On your way to join us at the Long Room, would you be so kind as to drop this off at the

Boston Gazette?" Adams handed Revere a piece of paper.

It was a notice which would appear in that newspaper the following day. It called upon the citizens of the towns surrounding Boston to come to a meeting at Faneuil Hall that Monday night.

Revere read it aloud:

"Every friend to his country, to himself, and to posterity is asked to attend to make a united and successful resistance to this last, worst, and most destructive measure of administration—the Tea Act and the arrival of the tea ship."

Paul Revere put the notice in his pocket.

"Thank you very much, Jeremy and Del," Mr. Adams said. "And good night to you both."

The boy and girl walked slowly home.

"Wouldn't you like to know what they are going to do tonight, Jeremy?" Del asked.

"Hmmmm," was Jeremy's reply.

"Do you think we could go? Mr. Adams said they would meet at the Long Room. Maybe we could slip in and hide?"

"It's Sunday night, Del. Father and Mother would never let us go out."

"Oh. That's right." There was disappointment in Del's voice.

As Del and Jeremy entered their home, their parents were just putting on their heavy Sunday cloaks.

"You're later than I thought you would be," their mother said.

"I don't like you to be out after dark," their father added. "Not in such times as these."

Neither Jeremy nor Del said anything.

"Your father and I are going out," Mistress Winthrop said. "You two have your supper and do your chores. We won't be long."

"Where are you going, Mother?" Del asked.

"Your father has some business matters to take up with Governor Hutchinson. It has been some time since I paid my respects to Mistress Hutchinson, so I am going along."

At the mention of Governor Hutchinson's name, Jeremy's heart leaped to his throat. A frown came over Del's face. Governor Hutchinson, although born in America, had accepted King George's appointment to be Governor of Massachusetts Bay Colony. He was hated by the Sons of

Liberty for the way he stood up for the King and Parliament.

To Jeremy and Del, Governor Hutchinson was the enemy. And their father was going to meet with him this very night! Just a few blocks away from the Governor's house there would be another meeting. A meeting at which Mr. Adams and his friends would discuss plans to keep Governor Hutchinson from carrying out the King's orders to have the tea chests on board the *Dartmouth* put ashore.

The door closed behind Giles and Prudence Winthrop. Jeremy's mind was made up.

"Hungry, Del?" he asked. When she shook her head, he continued, "About going to that meeting of Mr. Adams—"

"Oh, Jeremy, we dassent!" answered Del, reaching for her cloak.

"Don't forget your scarf, Mistress Make-Up-Your-Mind." Jeremy, with a mock gentlemanly bow, swung open the door, and Del swept out regally.

CHAPTER FIVE

A Plot Overheard

DEL and Jeremy moved swiftly and silently through Boston's narrow, crooked streets. They were on their way to the Long Room, a meeting place above Edes and Gill, the printing shop on Court Street. They had little to fear from Snipe's Guard now. It was getting late, time for the Guards' supper and a good mug of ale—too late for trying to capture a lad and a lass.

It was also true, they knew, that Snipe's men hated him almost as much as the Bostonians did. Having no taste for the lieutenant's orders, they would give up the hunt just as soon as they could. Nevertheless, Jeremy and Del kept a keen lookout as they walked along.

Jeremy and Del knew the print shop well. Its owners, Mr. Edes and Mr. Gill, were bold patriots. They published the *Boston Gazette,* which Samuel Adams used as if it were his own newspaper. Almost every day, either Jeremy or Del would drop into the *Gazette* with a letter or an article written by Mr. Adams. Mr. Adams' words were widely read, and made the *Gazette* an important paper, because it expressed Mr. Adams' ideas.

The Long Room, on the second floor of the print shop, had been given over as a rallying-point for the leaders of the independence movement.

Jeremy and Del slipped in a back door of the print shop.

"Be careful not to touch anything," Jeremy whispered. "There's ink over everything. Don't get any on your cloak."

Jeremy and Del made their way through the dark print shop to a rear stairway. Quietly they mounted the stairs which opened into a long, narrow room. A lantern hanging over the front stairway gave off a feeble light.

Del looked the room over carefully. There were a table and several chairs. A stove stood near the center of the room, a few logs beside it.

"I don't see any place where we can hide, Jeremy," Del said worriedly.

"I'll think of some place."

"Well, you'd better hurry," Del said. "I don't know whether you saw him or not. But as we were leaving our house, I saw Mr. Adams leave his. He ought to be here any minute."

"Crickety! Then we have no time to lose," Jeremy exclaimed.

His eyes searched the dimly lighted room, seeking a place where he and Del could conceal themselves. Both heard the sound at the same time; the sound of a door slamming downstairs.

"Someone's coming! What will we do?" Del's voice was panicky.

"Come on." Jeremy grabbed Del by the hand and raced back to the far end of the room, near the rear stairway. In one corner of the room was a pile of papers. These were the original drafts of posters and placards written by Sam Adams and members of his Committee. Once the Committee decided on the exact wording, the posters would be sent downstairs to be printed.

Often Del and Jeremy had helped distribute the posters. Some were tacked on the famous Liberty Tree, on the edge of the Common. This tree, a huge elm, had gotten its name about eight years before. At that time, a flagstaff had been raised

Some were tacked on the famous Liberty Tree

from the base of its trunk. The staff extended far above the tree's highest branches. Whenever a flag was hoisted on the staff, that was the signal calling the Sons of Liberty to action. Other posters were hung in public buildings, or in the shops of merchants who were friendly to the cause of liberty and not afraid to show it.

The posters were the only quick way to call people together for a meeting.

Tonight, though, the posters were to serve a different purpose. Del and Jeremy burrowed into them like two frightened mice. By rearranging a few of the larger posters, they covered themselves completely. They weren't very comfortable, but they were out of sight.

They weren't a moment too soon. Sam Adams came into the room, carrying a lantern. He was followed by Joseph Warren and Josiah Quincy. They were soon joined by Paul Revere, John Hancock, William Molineux, and other patriots who had pledged their lives to the cause of liberty.

The men seated themselves and the meeting started immediately. Sam Adams took charge.

"I am sure we are all agreed as to what course of action we must take," he began. "First, we must draw up a placard, calling our townsmen and neighbors to a meeting at Faneuil Hall."

"We'll call for a meeting before noon tomorrow," Warren said. "All agreed?"

A chorus of "Ayes" was the answer.

"John," Mr. Adams addressed Mr. Hancock, "will you and Paul draw up the placard? Use one of those old posters over there in the corner. Mr. Gill can print it up for us first thing in the morning."

Jeremy's and Del's hearts were pounding. They would surely be discovered when Mr. Hancock came over to the discarded placards. They heard Mr. Adams speak again.

"The meeting tomorrow will show that the people are with us. I know they will back us in refusing to permit the tea to be unloaded. But since we won't let it land, and the owners won't ship it back to England, what's to be done with it?"

It was then that Del and Jeremy heard the start of the plan for the most famous tea party in all history. Just whose idea it was, they couldn't say. They heard a voice ask, "Wonder how tea would mix with salt water?" They were so excited, they could never afterwards decide between themselves whether the voice was that of Adams, Hancock, Revere, Warren, or Quincy. As soon as the question was asked, the two children heard a low chuckle; then a laugh, then a roar of laughter as everyone present rocked back in his chair and let loose howls of gaiety.

The plan was to go aboard the *Dartmouth*, take the chests of tea from its hold, and dump them into the harbor! What a tea party!

When the laughter died down, the youngsters heard the group of men decide to have the "tea party" on Tuesday, just two days off.

"But what about the other two tea ships, Sam?" Hancock asked.

"There's no telling when they will arrive. And we can't wait. Unless we take some strong action now, the people may not stay with us. They want action. We must see that they get it."

"Aye. You're right, Sam," Joseph Warren said.

"Anything more to discuss now?" Quincy asked.

Del and Jeremy became tense when they overheard this question. They knew the meeting was just about over. Hancock and Revere would soon be coming over to their hiding place, moving discarded placards, hunting for one less used than the others, on which to write their notice of the meeting.

"Hist," Jeremy heard Del signal him.

"What is it?" he whispered.

"They'll find us," Del breathed. "I don't want Mr. Adams to catch us spying on him."

"Neither do I," Jeremy answered. "Keep perfectly still."

They were both very, very quiet. They had heard the footsteps of Hancock and Revere drawing near. Then they heard Hancock's voice.

"Here we are, Paul. Any of these ought to do. We don't need much space to write on. Just one sentence."

"Here's a fairly clean one back here," Revere said.

The youngsters probably would have gone undiscovered if Paul Revere hadn't happened to pick that one particular poster. As he moved it, a flimsy piece of paper slid from underneath it, and landed under the tip of Del's nose. Although still concealed, every time she breathed in, the paper pressed gently against her nose. When she breathed out, away the paper would go—a quarter

*They heard the plan for the most famous tea
party in all history*

of an inch. Del wrinkled her nose. She tried to hold her breath. But she couldn't. She pressed her finger hard against her upper lip. "Ah-ah-ah-choo!"

"What was that?" Hancock asked in a startled voice.

"I don't know. I'll see."

Revere leaned forward. Carefully he moved some of the papers aside. As he did so, he stared into two frightened eyes. Del's. Without saying a word, Revere slowly closed one of his eyes in a wink that said, "Don't worry, I won't give you away."

"Well, what is it, Paul?" Hancock asked, growing impatient.

"Mice," said Revere gravely.

"Mice! Sneezing mice! What are you talking about!" Hancock was now indignant.

This was too much for Del. First she started to giggle. She tried to stop. But trying to stop seemed to make it worse. Soon her giggle had grown into laughter that shook the posters covering her.

"Mice, eh? Powerful big ones they must be. Hey, Sam . . . look here!"

"Wait, John," Revere said. But it was too late.

80

Sam Adams was crossing the room. "It's the Winthrop children," Revere said hurriedly, just before Adams reached them.

"Sam," Hancock remarked, "it's been said that the words you write move people to action; they're moving words. Now do you want to see some of your words really move?"

With that, Hancock picked up a piece of kindling and started jabbing about the pile of papers. His aim was blind, but he struck vital spots. He caught Jeremy twice in the ribs. Del felt a jab on one elbow and then in the small of the back as she turned over to protect her face. Hancock continued his prodding, and suddenly, papers, placards, posters were flying toward the ceiling as Jeremy and Del leaped to their feet to escape Hancock's thrusts.

The rest of the Committee were gathered around laughing at the youngsters' discomfort.

Jeremy and Del stood silently, their heads hung in shame.

"We're sorry, sir," Jeremy said finally.

"I'm sure you are," Sam Adams said. "But that doesn't help. You two have overheard important plans here tonight. If the British were to learn—

if they were to know what you two know, it could mean death to our plan."

What was there to say? Del and Jeremy remained silent.

"It is too late to change our plan. I am going to ask that you swear silence about what you have heard. Will you swear to secrecy?"

"Oh, yes! We do! We do!" Del and Jeremy spoke as one.

"I feel sure I can trust you," Adams continued, "but you must most solemnly make your vow—as patriots."

With dignity, the boy and girl placed their right

hands on their hearts and swore not to reveal what they had overheard in the Long Room.

"I want you both to know that I am not at all pleased with your action tonight. You will go home now, at once," snapped Mr. Adams.

Del and Jeremy quickly left the room, and hurried home through the dark, quiet streets. They performed their chores quietly, neither saying much to the other. They were in their own rooms and in bed just before they heard their parents return.

Both were tired, but even in the few minutes it took them to fall into a sound sleep, puzzled thoughts ran through Jeremy's mind. He and Del were now sworn members of a group plotting a strong action against the Crown. Yet, their father had just come back from a visit to the Crown's representative in Massachusetts—Governor Hutchinson. Why—*why* wasn't their father helping the cause of liberty?

CHAPTER SIX

Stubbs Has Startling News

JEREMY and Del were thrilled the next morning when they joined the huge crowd trying to get into Faneuil Hall. Not only had they actually been at the meeting which had called this great crowd together, but they also knew something the crowd didn't know, and wasn't to know for some time yet. They knew what was going to happen to the tea.

Samuel Adams arose from among the hundreds of people crowded into the hall, and presented a proposal to be voted upon.

"As the towns have determined at a late meeting legally assembled that they will to the utmost of their power prevent the landing of the tea, the question be now put: whether this body are absolutely determined that the tea now arrived shall be returned to the place from whence it came."

Not a single person voted against this motion.

Del and Jeremy saw Samuel Adams nod his head at Josiah Quincy and Joseph Warren. They had been right. The people were behind them. The people wanted action, too. This was shown by the huge crowd which by now had grown so large that it was decided to move the meeting to Old South Meeting House, called the "Sanctuary of Freedom."

At Old South, Adams' motion was repeated with the addition: "Is it the firm resolution of this body that the tea shall not only be sent back but that no duty shall be paid thereon?"

Again, not a single person voted against the resolution.

Jeremy plucked Del by the sleeve.

"Come on. Let's go down to Griffin's Wharf."

The *Dartmouth,* with one hundred and fourteen chests of tea in her hold, had been brought in and moored to Griffin's Wharf earlier that morning.

Del and Jeremy strolled out on the wharf. Boston Harbor was a busy place. Ships from all over the world came and went each day. The brother and sister watched a three-masted schooner pull slowly away from India Wharf, just a few hundred feet beyond. The ship's crew was made up of brothers and fathers of playmates of Jeremy and Del. Right now, a number of them were on India Wharf, waving good-by to their loved ones. Many months would pass before they would see them again. The ship would sail the long, treacherous way around Cape Horn to India for its return cargo of spices, precious oils, and fine woods.

Years ago, before Jeremy and Del were born, Giles Winthrop had stood on India Wharf, waving good-by to his father, the first Jeremy Winthrop, captain of the schooner *Lightning,* India bound. Months went by before word reached Boston that the *Lightning* and all aboard her had perished in a typhoon in the China Sea.

Jeremy and Del approached the *Dartmouth's* gangplank. They stared up curiously at the ship, all sorts of thoughts running through their heads. There was tea in the *Dartmouth.* But it wasn't going to be there long. Jeremy grinned, looked at Del and saw a smile on her face. Evidently they both were thinking the same thing.

As they stood looking at the ship, a door in the forecastle swung open and they saw a Redcoat come out. They pressed forward for a better view, anxious to see who it was, curious as to why a British soldier should be on board the *Dartmouth*. There was no mistaking this Redcoat. It was their friend Sergeant Hubert Stubbs.

They watched as he made his way with land-lubber caution down the gangplank. Then the sergeant recognized them.

"Hullo, there. And how be the two of you?"

"We're fine, Sergeant," Jeremy answered. "What brings you to the *Dartmouth?*"

"Looking for a cup of tea?" Del asked laughingly.

"Aye. There's plenty of it in there. And fine tea it is. Bohea. The best. But I'm wonderin' how much of it, if any, will ever get to shore."

Jeremy and Del exchanged glances without speaking.

"But it wasn't tea I was after. No, sir. It was a packet of letters I am expectin'."

"And your mail didn't come?" Jeremy asked.

"No. And disappointed I am," Stubbs said.

"That's too bad," Del said sympathetically.

"That it is. But not completely hopeless. I'll just have to wait another day or two."

"What do you mean?" Jeremy asked. Quite often Stubbs let drop bits of information in his conversation without even realizing that what he was saying might be important.

"Why, just that the mail will be along in the *Eleanor* or the *Beaver* in a day or two."

"The other two tea ships?" Del asked.

"Right you are, lass."

"But they're not expected for some time. Maybe two or three weeks," Jeremy remarked innocently.

"Is that so?" Stubbs asked. "I'd like to know where you get your information. Maybe you get it from a better source than I get me own?"

"And where do you get yours?" Jeremy asked.

"From the master of the *Dartmouth,* Captain Hall himself. And who would know better?"

Who would? thought Jeremy. He'd better find out more about this. This was important.

"When does Captain Hall expect the other two ships?" Jeremy asked casually.

"Tomorrow, maybe, or the next day for sure."

Tomorrow! The very day that plans had been made to dump the tea from the *Dartmouth.* This would never do! The colonists would look silly if they dumped the tea from one ship, only to have two more ships arrive loaded with tea. Much better, much, much better, to wait for the *Beaver* and the *Eleanor* and dump all the tea. That is, if the other two ships were due to arrive so soon.

"Captain Hall could be mistaken, I suppose," Jeremy said most casually, as if he didn't have much faith in Captain Hall.

"Why do you say that, Jeremy?" Del said. She knew Jeremy was trying to draw out all the information he could from Sergeant Stubbs, and she wanted to help her brother.

"Oh, you know how sea captains are. Always talking as if they knew it all."

"Now lookee here, you two," Stubbs interrupted. "That's no way to be talkin' about a fine man like Captain Hall."

"What makes him so sure then?" Jeremy demanded.

"Why shouldn't he be sure? Who is more anxious for mail than myself? I'm pressin' Captain Hall just as you're pressin' me. I says to him, I says: 'Captain, sir, how kin ye be so sure the *Eleanor* and the *Beaver* is right behind ye?' And then he tells me how his ship was loaded first, and took advantage of the tide to leave. But he waited outside

the Thames for the *Beaver* and *Eleanor* to catch
up. They held the mail for the last ship to leave,
to bring all they could. That's why Captain Hall
hasn't none, and it's all on the *Beaver* or the
Eleanor."

"But just because three ships leave together
doesn't mean they always arrive together," Jeremy
still protested.

"Right you are, lad. But not this time. Nope.
The three stayed in sight of each other all the way
across. Afeered of pirates, maybe. Captain Hall
told me he last saw the other two ships evenin'
afore last—Saturday that would be. They parted
company just off Providence, Rhode Island. The
Beaver had a small cargo to land there, and the
Eleanor must have gone in with the *Beaver* to drop
off some mail."

This made sense now. Jeremy and Del looked
at one another. They both knew they had important news; news that must reach Mr. Sam Adams
without delay. This news would change lots of
plans.

"Yup. I expect the other two to sail into harbor
in the morning. Bringin' me some mail from me
family, I hope."

Sergeant Stubbs shook his head in bewilderment

Jeremy did some rapid figuring. From what he knew of sailing ships, he thought the sergeant must be just about right in his timing of the arrival of the other two ships. They would have to put into Narragansett Bay for Providence. In and out would take a full day at least, depending on the winds and tides. Then they would have to come around Cape Cod to come into Boston. All in all, the stop-off at Providence would use up just about two days.

That would mean, then, that the *Eleanor* and the *Beaver* might sail into Boston Harbor at the very moment the tea from the *Dartmouth* was being dumped into the harbor.

Certainly that would never do!

Jeremy and Del said good-by to Sergeant Stubbs.

"And thank you, Sergeant. Thank you very much," Jeremy couldn't help adding.

"Thank me? For what?" the sergeant asked, puzzled.

"For helping us have a much bigger party than we expected to have. Bye!"

The children were off, leaving Sergeant Stubbs staring after them, shaking his head in bewilderment.

CHAPTER SEVEN

Del Disappears

DEL and Jeremy felt pretty good about themselves as they hurried along toward Mr. Sam Adams' house. They felt they had done a good job that morning. The information they had gotten out of Sergeant Stubbs was important. There was no doubt about that.

"I'm awfully glad we went down to Griffin's Wharf," Del said to her brother.

"I am too. Mr. Adams and the Committee are going to be glad of the information we have. They'll make new plans now. I'm sure they will want to wait until the *Eleanor* and the *Beaver* arrive before holding their tea party."

Del laughed at the way Jeremy said, "tea party."

"Yes," Del replied. "And maybe now Mr.

Adams will forget that he was vexed with us last night for slipping into that meeting."

"We'd better go right to his house before we go home to dinner, hadn't we?" Jeremy asked.

"I think so," Del agreed.

But their father had other ideas. As they were about to pass their own house, they heard Mr. Winthrop call.

"Come into the house. Right away," he ordered.

Dinner was already on the table. As they ate, very little was said. Usually their dinners were gay, filled with laughter and conversation. Not today, however. Apparently Giles Winthrop had something on his mind. So did Jeremy and Del. Both were wondering how quickly they could leave the house and deliver their news to Mr. Adams. Both were thinking also of their father's visit the night before to Governor Hutchinson.

Del and Jeremy finished, and asked to be excused.

"Just a minute," their father said. "Jeremy, go into my study. I'll follow in a minute. I want to talk to you."

Jeremy looked at Del and frowned. Del raised her eyebrows questioningly, as if to ask her brother if she should go on over to see Mr. Adams. Jeremy shook his head ever so slightly.

It seemed that Mr. Winthrop was reading his children's thoughts. "I want you to stay in the house, too, Del," he said firmly.

Mr. Winthrop watched Del enter the kitchen, then followed his son.

Jeremy sat in his father's study, waiting impatiently for him to speak. Finally Mr. Winthrop, after carefully straightening some paper, lighted his pipe and leaned forward.

"I'm afraid, son," Mr. Winthrop began, "that you have become much too wrapped up in the af-

fairs of the day. I can understand how exciting it must be to you and your sister. You are associating with important people. But I'm afraid that what they are doing is something quite different from what a fourteen-year-old boy should be doing."

"But, Father, I'm—"

"Just a minute. Let me finish. Many people in the last few days have told me of the escapades you and your sister have become involved in. You've had several brushes with the British Guard. That can be dangerous."

"We can take care of ourselves, Father."

"Mmmm. That remains to be seen. At any rate, I can't have you worrying your mother, and endangering your own life and that of your sister. Both of you also have been staying out too late at night. You have more free time than other boys your age, because I myself teach you, and you are not confined by school sessions. However, I cannot permit you and your sister to run wild. Indeed, I'm going to demand that you put a halt to your activities."

"But, Father," Jeremy pleaded, "we can't. We just can't stop now. You don't know what you're asking."

"I think I do. And believe me, Jeremy, I have thought this over carefully. Now, I don't want either of you to leave the house this afternoon. I'm going over to the college. When I return, I shall examine your Latin lessons. I'd advise you to spend the rest of the afternoon studying. Del is to busy herself with all the family mending. You may go now."

Jeremy was furious. It wasn't fair! Now the boy was convinced that his father was on the side of the enemy. But how could he be! How *could* his father side with the British?

Jeremy, his face reddened with anger at his father's orders for the day, signaled Del to follow him to his room upstairs.

"Shut the door and sit down," he barked at her.

For once, Del quietly obeyed. It wasn't often she saw her brother as angry as he was now. She knew that the best thing to do was to remain silent and let him work it out.

"Father says we are not to go out of the house this afternoon," Jeremy told her.

"No! Jeremy, he can't have! What about Mr. Adams and the news of the other ships?"

Jeremy shook his head. "I don't know what's got into Father lately. But we must figure some way of getting the message over to Mr. Adams."

The children sat quietly, their brows furrowed with thought. Suddenly Jeremy got up, crossed the room, and stared out of his window. There was Mr. Adams' house, only a few hundred feet away. It might as well have been a mile.

As he looked out the window, he saw his father walking up the street, in the direction of Harvard College. It never occurred to Jeremy, though, nor to Del either, deliberately to disobey and go to the Adams house despite their father's orders.

"Jeremy, did Father say we just had to stay in this *afternoon?*" Del asked.

"Yes. But you know what he meant. He meant we weren't to help Mr. Adams any more."

There was a sly look on Del's face.

"But Jeremy— Father *said,* 'afternoon,' didn't he?"

Jeremy looked at his sister. Del went right on.

"He *didn't* say anything about tonight."

Jeremy knew what Del was getting at. If they followed Del's idea, they would have a mighty weak excuse if their father were to find out. Yet what else could they do? A slight, determined grin came over Jeremy's face.

"All right, Del. Father did say this afternoon—not tonight. We'll do it. Now let's get our work done so when Father comes home he won't suspect anything."

The Latin test Giles Winthrop gave Jeremy when he came home went off perfectly. And piles of neatly mended stockings, waistcoats, and breeches mended by Del were ready for his inspection. Their father complimented them. Supper went off smoothly. Nothing was said about Mr. Adams, or the British, or the tea ships. The children carefully kept the talk away from any subject that might start more conversation such as Jeremy had had with his father earlier that afternoon.

Shortly after supper, the dishes done, brother and sister said good night to their parents and went upstairs to their rooms.

Outside Jeremy's room, they stopped. Jeremy, in a low voice, said to Del:

"Now listen to me, Sis. This is something I must do by myself. Please don't argue with me. After what Father said to me, I know I must not let you take any more risks. Here's what I am going to do. I'm going to slip out of my window, climb down the elm tree, and hurry over to Mr. Adams' house. I'm sure I can do this and be back before you are even undressed for bed."

Jeremy cut Del's protests short by entering his room and closing the door. He waited a few minutes, then cautiously opened his window. It squeaked loudly. Jeremy stood frozen, listening. When he heard no sound of someone approaching, he sat astride the window sill. A huge limb from an old elm tree near by touched the side of the house. In the summer, when the tree was in full leaf, the leaves often brushed against his window, making a weird, scratchy sound.

Carefully Jeremy eased out of his window. His right foot found a firm place on the tree branch. He pushed out from the side of the house, and grabbed for another limb. He made it. He was safely in the tree. He rested a moment, then slowly, quietly, began his descent.

Jeremy's feet touched the ground. He congratulated himself on how easy it had been—

"You may return to your room now, Jeremy. I'll talk to you about this in the morning." Giles

"You may return to your room now, Jeremy"

Winthrop's voice came out of the night. Standing by the side of the house, he had been watching Jeremy's silent descent. Jeremy looked at his father briefly, turned, and ran back into the house, tears stinging his eyes.

Outside of Del's room he paused. He'd have to tell her of his failure.

"Del," he called softly. "Del." There was no answer. Asleep already, he thought. Shows how much she really cares whether I got to see Mr. Adams or not.

Jeremy turned the knob of his sister's door. Slowly he opened it, and looked in. He blinked his eyes, getting them used to the dark. Del was not in bed, nor moving about the room. He entered, calling softly for his sister. There was no answer.

Del was gone.

CHAPTER EIGHT

Cannon Are Loaded

JEREMY stretched out on his bed without un-
dressing. He didn't know what to do. He didn't
know what he *could* do. How had Del learned that
he had failed in his attempt to slip down the tree
and get to Mr. Adams' house? How had *she* man-
aged to get out of the house? He didn't have the
answers. All he knew was that Del was gone.

In his troubled mind, every noise in the still
night seemed to be magnified a hundred times. His
ears strained to catch any sound that might tell
him Del was near by, and safe. He thought of trying to go out again, to search for her. If he did,
though, he reasoned, and was again caught by his
father, he would give Del away. No, the best thing
was to wait awhile longer. If Del didn't return
soon he'd have to go out and look for her, even if
it meant telling his father.

His ears caught the faint sound of a downstairs door closing. A moment later, he heard a rustle. In the pale November moonlight, he saw a piece of white paper sliding under his door. He heard the door to Del's room closing as he picked up the paper. Jeremy crossed to his window, and in the light of the moon read a message, hastily scribbled in Del's handwriting:

"Delivered message to Mr. A. Tell you about it in the morning."

Jeremy gave a sigh of relief, undressed, and got into bed.

His sleep that night was a restless one. Weird dreams romped through his mind. In one of them, he was climbing down a tree. He looked down and there on the ground below stood a large bear, its teeth bared, huge paws outstretched to grab him. The dream shifted, and now Jeremy was halfway up the mast of the *Dartmouth*. Again he was trying to descend. There was Queue, in the red coat of a British soldier, snarling up at him. His friend Queue!

Jeremy awoke with a start. He shuddered. It was just growing daylight. His dream had been so real that he half expected to see Queue, dressed as a Lobsterback, come padding across the room. Then he grinned, half ashamed of himself, buried his head in the pillow, and tried to get a few more winks of sleep before he would have to get up.

At breakfast that morning, the expression on Del's face told Jeremy she was mighty pleased with herself. She smirked at him several times, and when their father joined them at the table, quickly put her finger to her lips for silence. As if he, Jeremy, would say anything! What cheek! He'd fix her! But then, he had to admit she had gotten the message to Mr. Adams where he had failed.

It was also strange, Jeremy thought, that his father said nothing at all about his disobedience. Jeremy had been wondering fearfully what punishment might be due.

What Jeremy didn't know, nor did Del, was that their mother and father had had quite a lengthy conversation that morning. It wasn't often that Mistress Winthrop interfered when her husband disciplined the children. When she did, he listened, and took her advice.

Breakfast continued as if nothing unusual had happened in the past twenty-four hours. When everyone had finished, the children put on their cloaks and went out into the yard.

As soon as Jeremy was alone with Del, he demanded an explanation.

"How did you get out last night?" Jeremy asked.

"Wouldn't you like to know?" Del teased.

"Now you look here, Del. You tell me, or I'll—I'll—"

"You'll what? And you look here! Who got the message about the ships to Mr. Adams? Did you? Un—uh! It took a girl to do it."

"All right! All right! But how?"

Del smiled. "Well," she said slowly, "knowing you'd be so clumsy that you'd get caught, I knew I'd have to do it. So—I rigged up a breeches buoy, got in, and pulleyed myself across—"

"Oh, stop the nonsense, Sis!" Jeremy cut in.

Del laughed. "Really, Jeremy, it was the greatest stroke of luck."

"What do you mean?"

"Well," Del continued, "I was just starting to get undressed when Mother knocked at my door. She said Father had just stepped out—on his way out to catch you, I suppose—and would I do her a favor."

"Yes, yes . . . go on," Jeremy said impatiently.

"She asked me to take a recipe over to Mistress Adams. She said it *could* wait until morning, but then perhaps Mistress Adams would want to start making the pudding very early, so would I mind going over in the dark.

"Oh, Jeremy, it was such good fortune that I could scarcely hold our news back." Del gave

Jeremy a sidelong glance, her head held sheepishly against her shoulder.

Jeremy knew *that* look. Del had spilled the beans without meaning to.

"Del, you . . . you tattler! Did you tell Mother we *had* to see Mr. Adams?"

"Word of honor, I didn't," insisted Del, her dark eyes straight upon her brother. "All I said was, 'But Jeremy has already—' and Mother cut me short. Then she said the queerest thing. She said, 'The bird in the tree is about to be caught. Little birds can't tell if they're caught, can they?' " Del's eyes were suddenly twinkling.

Jeremy gave a whoop of laughter.

"By the sacred cod! That squeaky window in my room! Mother told me to beeswax it the other day, but I forgot. She must have heard it open and put two and two together."

"But, Jeremy," said Del, still puzzled. "How could Mother have known we had a message for Mr. Adams?"

"She couldn't have, goose. She probably just guessed something was in the air, and decided one of us should see Mr. Adams. And with Father angry . . ." Jeremy finished lamely.

"I think I know what you mean. Sometimes I have the feeling Mother's more on our side than— than on Father's," Del said in a low voice, swallowing the lump in her throat.

Troubled by the thought Del had put into words, both youngsters sat silent.

The news Del had taken Mr. Adams about the expected arrival of the *Beaver* and the *Eleanor* stirred him to instant action. Mr. Adams had sent his servant, Surry, to fetch Paul Revere. Revere had spent most of the night on horseback, riding to the homes of members of the Committee of Correspondence. He told them of the change in plans, and had summoned them to a meeting at the North End Club to be held the first thing in the morning.

At the very moment the meeting was taking place, Del and Jeremy were on their way to Griffin's Wharf. They arrived there just in time to see the *Beaver* and the *Eleanor* sail into the harbor. They stood on the dock and watched the two ships come slowly alongside the wharf and tie up next to the *Dartmouth*. A large crowd had gathered. The children saw Sergeant Stubbs. He was there hoping to receive mail from his loved ones back in England, as were many others. Some, though, were anxious to find out for certain if these ships also carried tea in their holds.

Jeremy and Del pressed closer into the crowd. They, too, wanted to know about this. They found out from Sergeant Stubbs. Stubbs was not his usual cheerful self. He was quite serious.

"Aye," he told them, "they're both carrying tea. Now there's three ships here with it, and none of 'em allowed to land the tea. You two want to be mighty careful. No tellin' what will happen now."

Del and Jeremy had just started to leave the wharf when a great shout went up.

"Look! Look!" the crowd yelled.

The two children quickly spotted what was causing the commotion.

Two British battleships, the men-of-war *Active* and *Kingfisher,* had swung into the channel just

opposite Griffin's Wharf. Sailors aboard the two ships could be seen loading shot into the warships' cannons.

Jeremy and Del looked at one another. What could this mean? For the first time, they felt fear.

CHAPTER NINE

Slipping Aboard

EXCITEMENT in Boston ran higher and higher as the days slipped swiftly by. Two weeks had passed since the *Dartmouth* had dropped her hook in Boston Harbor. People knew that the British men-of-war *Active* and *Kingfisher* had been moved into the channel just off Griffin's Wharf on orders of Admiral Montague. Had his orders for this warlike gesture come from Governor Hutchinson? The cannon of the two warships were trained on the tea ships. They were loaded with shot. Would they actually be fired if the patriots tried to prevent the landing of the tea?

These were the questions burning in the hearts and minds of all the Sons of Liberty. These were the questions which would have to be answered, and answered soon.

The revenue laws of the British Government

said that the cargo of any ship must be unloaded within twenty days of its arrival in port. If this was not done, then the ship was to be taken from its owners, and its cargo unloaded under the protection of the British warships. That was why the

Active and the *Kingfisher* had their loaded broadsides trained on Griffin's Wharf. If the patriots should try to stop the landing of the tea, they would be raked by hot shot from the warships' guns.

Not a day passed that a new poster or a new

placard wasn't hung from the Liberty Tree. One of them read:

THE TEA SHALL NOT BE LANDED AT THE RISK OF OUR LIVES AND OUR PROPERTIES.

Just below this poster there hung another which said in bold letters:

SHOW ME THE MAN THAT DARES TAKE THIS DOWN.

At another jam-packed meeting in Old South, one patriot urged caution. He suggested further meetings with the Governor. He was shouted down as the people in the meeting cried out, "Our hands have been put to the plow! We must not look back! The tea shall not be landed!"

The days sped by.

Del and Jeremy were kept busy running errands and hanging up posters. Their father had remained strangely silent. He had not again ordered them to stop their activities. They didn't question him about it. They thought it wiser to go about their exciting duties without discussing the matter.

Then one evening, as they were returning home, they passed the Governor's mansion. Del grabbed Jeremy by the sleeve of his coat.

"Jeremy! Look!"

Jeremy turned his head in the direction Del was pointing.

"Isn't that Father?" she asked.

Jeremy and Del slipped behind a tree. They watched the man for a moment. Then Jeremy nodded his head. There could be no doubt. It was their father.

They watched him as he cautiously looked about, as if to see if he were being observed. Then, quickly, he ducked into a side entrance of the Governor's mansion.

Jeremy's and Del's hearts sank. Both had to fight back the tears which were filling their eyes.

"Why, Del? Why!" Jeremy asked sadly.

Del could only shake her head.

Jeremy and Del trudged slowly home, low in spirits, troubled in mind. In front of their house, Jeremy turned to his sister.

"Del, I've just got to find out what's going on. There must be some important reason for Father to be visiting the Redcoats at this time. Some-

They watched as he ducked into a side entrance

thing's about to happen. Something important. I think I know how I can find out."

"How, Jeremy? How?"

"Sis," Jeremy said slowly, "I'm going to sneak aboard the *Dartmouth*. If they're getting ready to unload the tea, there will be talk about it. You know it has to be unloaded in a few days or the ships will be seized, and they'll unload it by force."

"I'll go with you, and stand lookout."

"No, you won't. I'm going to do this by myself. It's kind of risky. Oh, I don't mean there's any real danger, but, crickety, Sis, this is no job for a girl."

"All right, Jeremy," Del said meekly. Jeremy didn't notice that she agreed *too* meekly. Already he was hurrying down Purchase Street on his way to Griffin's Wharf.

Del waited about five minutes, then hurried after her brother.

At the wharf, Jeremy watched two Redcoats walk their guard posts. One would start from one end of the dock, the other from the opposite end. They would meet precisely at the gangplank of the *Dartmouth*, about face, and retrace their steps. Jeremy waited until the guards were farthest from the ship's gangplank, then he darted onto the ship.

Once aboard, he ducked behind a stack of chests and waited. No one seemed to be stirring. Quietly, carefully, he made his way along the ship's deck until he reached the captain's cabin. He ducked inside.

In the dim light from a whale-oil lamp, he looked about him. Jeremy didn't know what he expected to find, but he hoped there might be something that would give him a clue as to what the *Dartmouth's* Captain Hall planned to do.

Suddenly he heard voices, then footsteps. He slipped behind the captain's huge sea chest. He was out of sight when Captain Hall and the captains of the other two tea ships entered the cabin.

"Thank you, Captain, for an excellent repast," one of the officers was saying.

"Before you return to your ships, you'll join me in a mug of rum, won't you?" Captain Hall invited.

"With pleasure, sir."

"I always say there's nothing to top off a good meal like a good tot of grog."

"Better than a spot of tea?" Captain Hall asked.

The other two captains joined him in a roar of laughter.

"Speaking of tea—are you going to let 'em take your ship?" one asked.

"Take my ship?" Captain Hall roared. "Not I! I've fought off pirates in my day. No whining colonists or weak-kneed soldiers will board Captain Hall's ship!"

"But what will you do?"

"Never fear. I have a plan. Here, another mug of rum all around."

Jeremy, shaking with fright, afraid of being discovered any minute, heard the gurgle of the liquid as it was poured into the cups. Sometimes the voices of the three men became so low, Jeremy could barely make out snatches of the conversation. Twice more the cups were filled with rum. As the rum flowed, the voices became less guarded, and Jeremy heard Captain Hall describe his plan.

"On the twentieth day, mind you, the day before it's legal for them to seize this ship, I plan to unload this tea in the dead of night, pull up my anchor, and set sail for England. You'll be wise to do the same."

There was a pause, as the other captains let the plan sink into their minds.

"A good plan, Captain. I'll do the same. What about you, James?"

"I'm with you."

"Then let's drink to it."

Again the cups were filled. The men drank in silence.

"Now, Captain, we must say good night and get back to our ships."

"Not a word about our plan, mind you," Captain Hall commanded.

"Mum's the word," the others answered, and left the cabin.

Jeremy waited. How was he going to get out of the cabin? Captain Hall made no move to retire to his bunk. He sat silently sipping rum. After what seemed like hours to Jeremy, he heard a thin little sound. A snore? Jerry thought hopefully. The faint snore rose in volume, fell, only to grow and grow until the captain's snores rocked the cabin.

Jeremy came out of his hiding place. He looked at the captain, whose head was thrown back in his chair while gusty snores came from his open mouth.

"A champion at snoring, this one," Jeremy decided. He had reached the door of the cabin when, suddenly, an ear-splitting howl soared above the booming of the captain's snores.

Jeremy had stepped on the tail of the captain's cat.

CHAPTER TEN

Paleface Redskins

D EL reached Griffin's Wharf only seconds after Jeremy slipped aboard the *Dartmouth*. She pressed back against a large piling, her dark cloak blending with it, making her almost unnoticeable.

The minutes dragged by. No sign of Jeremy. Del knew it was growing late. Her stomach told her. Neither she nor Jeremy had eaten supper.

The position she was in grew more and more uncomfortable. She shifted slightly to ease her back. She watched the Lobsterbacks pace their posts. To pass time, she counted the number of steps it took them to walk up the dock and back. It took just seventy paces for each. Del figured that if it took about one second to take one step, then the soldiers walked up and back about every two minutes.

She would let them go up and back five more times—ten minutes—then she would go for help if Jeremy hadn't returned. For all she knew, he might be a prisoner on board the ship.

Once, she counted . . . twice, three times . . . four . . . five . . . and she was off, running swiftly toward home.

Whom could she ask for help? Her father? No. Her mother? Could a girl and a woman accomplish anything against a ship full of dangerous sailors? Del's imagination pictured fantastic seamen aboard the *Dartmouth,* crazed, bloodthirsty pirates, knives in their teeth, cutlasses in their scarred hands.

Her wild thoughts raced with her feet. Suddenly, she saw Surry, Mr. Adams' able servant, turning into the Adams house, back from a visit to a fisherman friend. Under her arm she held a huge codfish loosely wrapped in paper. With her was Queue.

"Oh, Surry! Could you help me?" Quickly Del explained the trouble she feared Jeremy to be in. Surry never hesitated.

"Come on, Miss Deliverance. We'll get your brother."

Off they went. Behind them, like a big dark shadow, followed Queue.

They raced onto the wharf just in time to hear

loud shouts break out across the still, moonlit night.

"There he goes. Stop him! Stop him!"

Del saw Jeremy come scampering down the *Dartmouth's* gangplank. From the two ends of the wharf, the Redcoat guards came running. Several men were dashing off the ship in hot pursuit of Jeremy.

As a guard running from the land end of the wharf closed in, Surry hurled her package at his head—and missed. The newspaper flew open and the huge codfish slithered under the Redcoat's feet. The fat fish squooshed under one foot and the soldier went skidding across the wharf. Plop! He lay sprawled on his back, leaving the entrance to the wharf clear for Jeremy's escape.

Queue raced by and was quickly in the thick of the oncoming sailors. He held them up long enough for Jeremy to grab Del's hand, and off they went.

"Come on, Surry," Del cried out. "We're all right now."

Just as they left the wooden planks of the dock, Jeremy stumbled and fell forward. As he sprawled out on hands and knees, something hurtled through the air, passing just over his head. Jeremy heard it strike the cobblestones of the street just in front of him. It was a belaying pin, the thick wooden spike used to secure ropes. It had been a lucky tumble. The murderous pin would have struck him full force on the back of his head.

He scrambled to his feet quickly with the aid of Surry's helping hand, and in a few minutes the three were safe. Once they were off the dock, the sailors gave up the chase. Queue was still keeping them busy.

"Surry, you were such a help! Thank you," Del cried. "But your poor fish! What will Mr. Adams have for dinner tomorrow?"

"Don't you worry yourself about that, child. Mr. Adams won't care, once he knows that fish turned a Redcoat upside-down, slantwise, sidewise, and every other kind of wise."

The three of them chuckled gleefully and said good night.

Once home, the children's mother hurried them quickly off to bed, saying, "I'll bring you up some bread and milk."

Better an early bedtime than Father's anger! Mother certainly *did* know best.

With warm, heavily buttered bread and milk stowed away, Jeremy and Del fell sound asleep immediately after their long and active day. Neither of them knew that when their father reached home, shortly afterward, he came to their rooms, tucked the covers around them, and softly caressed their heads with his gentle hand.

The next morning, right after breakfast, Jeremy and Del set out to find Mr. Adams and tell him of Captain Hall's plan.

They located Mr. Adams, along with other members of his Committee, at the North End Club. There they made a full report.

The children's mother hurried them off to bed

"So that's Captain Hall's plan, is it?" Mr. Adams said. "He would defy not only the colonists, but the Governor as well . . . but I wonder . . ."

"Wonder what, Sam?" Joseph Warren asked the question.

"Could it not be that Hall and Hutchinson have worked out this plan together? With the tea unloaded on the dock, and Hall gone, Hutchinson could deny any part in the tea's being landed. He could blame it all on Captain Hall. But the tea would have been unloaded, nevertheless. Hutchinson would have won out, despite everything we colonists have been threatening to do to stop it."

"Then we'll have to move before Hall does, Sam," Josiah Quincy said.

"You're right. We'll hold our tea party the night of the nineteenth day from the date of the *Dartmouth's* arrival. Just a day ahead of Captain Hall's plan to remove the tea."

"That would be the sixteenth," Paul Revere said.

"Day after tomorrow," Jeremy spoke up.

"Yes," Mr. Adams replied. "Thursday, December 16th—a date that may make history."

"You know, Sam, getting aboard those tea ships

isn't going to be too easy." It was John Hancock speaking. "There will be danger, too, if any of us are identified. We'll be subject to arrest under the King's warrant, if any of us are spotted."

"True, true."

Suddenly Del was bursting with excitement. She had an idea, a suggestion she just had to make.

"Mr. Adams," Del blurted out.

"Yes, Del?"

"Why don't you dress up like Indians with feathers, and painted faces. You could wear old blankets—there are still lots of Indians around. No one would ever recognize you."

The men of the Committee laughed. Then they became silent, thinking.

"A capital idea," Warren said. "Shall we accept the young lady's excellent suggestion, gentlemen?"

Del was entranced. *She* had been called a "young lady"!

A chorus of "Ayes" came from the Committee members.

"We'll do it just as you suggested, Del," Mr. Adams said.

"And just where will we get these disguises?" William Molineux cut in.

"Oh, don't worry about that, sir," Del said hastily. "Jeremy and I and our friends can get them. We can borrow blankets, get the feathers, and make some dye. I'm sure we can, can't we, Jeremy?"

"I know we can," Jeremy answered.

"You'll have to be quick," Mr. Adams said. "Today is Tuesday. Can you have everything ready by tomorrow night? We'll need about fifty sets of disguises."

Jeremy and Del nodded their heads.

"We can assemble them in separate bundles in the hayloft of our barn," Del said.

"Capital!" Hancock said. "And each man who is going to board the tea ships will come for his costume. Be sure they don't fall into the wrong hands."

"We ought to have a password." Jeremy was fired with plans. "We won't give a bundle to anyone who doesn't have the password."

All the men in the Committee were smiling. They had been caught up in the children's excitement.

"And what will the password be?" Adams asked.

Jeremy and Del looked at one another, their brows creased in deep thought.

"It ought to be something about tea," Jeremy said. "The tea on those ships is called Bohea," he added thoughtfully.

"I've got it," Del cried out. "No Bohea for Boston! That'll be the password—No Bohea for Boston!"

Laughter and the new chant rocked the room. *"No Bohea for Boston. No Bohea for Boston."*

Del and Jeremy arose, anxious to be off to round up their friends, and collect the material for the disguises.

"Jeremy," Mr. Adams said. "I wonder if you could do one thing more for me. It's this: could you find out when Captain Hall lets his men leave the ship for their nightly shore leave? I know it's somewhere around five o'clock. It would be better if the ships are boarded when there are as few of the crew on board as possible."

Jeremy gulped. To return to Griffin's Wharf so soon after what had happened last night could be dangerous. But the boy faced Mr. Adams squarely.

"Yes, sir. I'll find out," he promised.

CHAPTER ELEVEN

Feathers, Blankets, and Beets

THE rest of the day was a busy one for the Winthrop children. Jeremy, renamed "Chief Pluck-a-Feather," would gather his tribe. Del would collect blankets and get coloring material to stain faces red.

"Rebecca will help me, I know," Del said. "I can get Mercy and Bridget, too."

"All right, but remember, we haven't much time."

"Don't you fret about me. You just get the feathers. Where are you going to get them?"

"Never you mind. I'll get them."

"And what about getting that information for Mr. Adams? About when the sailors leave the ships?"

Jeremy frowned. "I'll have to go down there late

this afternoon. Maybe I'd better put on an Indian disguise."

Del laughed. "They may not be ready by then. But we'll have to get them done by tonight. Scoot. Get those feathers."

It was late afternoon when the brother and sister saw one another again.

Jeremy and his friend Timothy, each with a bag of feathers slung over their shoulders, were heading for the Winthrop barn. They were passing the Adams house just as Mr. Adams came out. He approached the two boys, and in a low, secret-spy voice, asked Jeremy about the feathers.

"We have them, sir. Look." Jeremy opened his bag. It was filled with long, beautiful turkey feathers.

"A fine haul, Jeremy. Just fine. Where did you get them?" Mr. Adams asked.

"At Governor Hutchinson's turkey farm, out in Milton, sir."

"What! Did you say Governor Hutchinson's farm?"

"Yes, sir."

Mr. Adams started laughing. His laughter grew until he was doubled over. Jeremy could still hear his guffaws as Mr. Adams walked down the street.

Jeremy had never seen the man so relaxed, so carefree, as if the weight of his great problems had been lifted momentarily from his shoulders.

In the Winthrop barn, up in the hayloft, Del and her friends were busily sewing away on pieces of old blankets. They cut oblongs long enough to cover a man's body, front and back. They stitched two pieces together, leaving an opening so that the blanket could be slipped over the head quickly, covering the body but leaving the arms free for action.

The girls were surrounded by dozens of small bottles.

"Where'd you get all those little bottles?" Jeremy asked.

"That was our hardest job," Del answered. "But fortunately we remembered that Mercy's uncle is an apothecary, and he let us have them."

"What's that stuff in them?"

Del laughed. "If I tell you, you have to promise not to tell Mother."

Jeremy nodded his head.

"It's beet juice. Mother gave it to us, but she doesn't know it."

For weeks afterwards, every time Mrs. Winthrop went to her cellar, she still puzzled over the disappearance of dozens of jars of beets she had so carefully preserved that fall.

Jeremy and Timothy dumped out their bags of feathers. Appreciative coos of delight came from the girls.

Hurriedly the children assembled the bundles. Into each blanket went a vial of beet juice, to color the face and hands. Along with it went eight carefully selected feathers. Then the blanket was rolled up and stacked neatly into a growing pile, near a chute which was intended to slide hay down to the horses below.

It was growing dark. Jeremy had to leave the others to return to Griffin's Wharf.

About an hour later Mistress Adams answered a knock on her back door. Puzzled, she entered her husband's study.

"Samuel, there's an Indian at the rear door. He wants to see you."

"An Indian to see me?"

Mistress Adams nodded her head.

"Well, I can't imagine who he is, but I'll see him." Mr. Adams left his study and made his way to the rear of the house. He opened the door cautiously.

"Yes? You wanted to see me?" he asked.

"Ugh."

"Come now, my friend, what is it you want?" Mr. Adams said, somewhat impatiently.

"Ugh. You not recognize heap big me?"

"Ugh. You not recognize heap big me?"

"No, I don't," Mr. Adams replied. "And I am quite busy. Please state what you want."

"It's me, sir. Jeremy. Honest, didn't you know me?"

For the second time that day, Mr. Adams had a good laugh.

"I certainly didn't, Jeremy. You fooled me completely."

"Well," Jeremy said, "I wanted to see if our disguises would work. And sir, the sailors were leaving the ships right after the bell in Old South tolled off five o'clock. Good night, sir."

"Good night, Jeremy, and thank you." Mr. Adams re-entered his study, chuckling.

Jeremy had kept his fingers crossed as he told this half-truth. He didn't say that not a single sailor had been suspicious of the funny-looking Indian loitering on the wharf.

CHAPTER TWELVE

"No Bohea for Boston!"

THE next day Jeremy and Del attended a meeting of the Committee of Correspondence to receive final instructions. Mr. Adams and other members of the Committee had come to rely more and more on the brother and sister to help them carry out the details of their plans.

It was decided that, beginning at seven o'clock that night, Jeremy and Del would be in the hayloft of their barn to pass out the bundles of Indian disguises. Mr. Adams, thinking of the children's safety, thought it best that Jeremy and Del remain in the loft, ready to slide a disguise down the hay-chute whenever they heard a voice call, "No Bohea for Boston!"

In this way, neither Jeremy nor Del would know to whom they passed a bundle. In the event the British learned of the children's participation in the tea party, they could truthfully say they knew no one.

Details were straightened out. On Thursday, the day scheduled for dumping the tea, a huge meeting was to be held in Old South. Jeremy was not to attend the meeting. He was to station himself at the entrance to Griffin's Wharf. The moment he saw the sailors leave the tea ships, he was to race to Old South, and signal to Del. Del was to find a place inside the meeting house as near to Mr. Adams as possible. On getting the signal from Jeremy that the sailors had left the ships, she was to pass it on to Mr. Adams. He then would pronounce the words, already agreed upon, which would send the patriots to Griffin's Wharf to board the tea ships.

Wednesday night, right after supper, Jeremy and Del went out to the barn. Their father said nothing about their leaving. He didn't even ask them where they were going. Strange indeed, but Father's actions were *all* peculiar these days, the children thought.

They climbed the ladder to the hayloft. They didn't have long to wait. Within a few minutes after they took their positions at the top of the hay-

Del and her friends were busily sewing

chute, they heard a voice say, "No Bohea for Boston!"

Del giggled. Jeremy shushed her. She handed him a bundle, and down the chute it went.

For the next half hour they were busy. Time after time, they heard the secret phrase, and down the chute would go another bundle.

One voice puzzled them. It was a high-pitched voice. It sounded as if it were a man trying to talk like a woman, as if he didn't want his real voice to be recognized.

Del whispered to Jeremy, "Isn't that funny? Why would anybody talk like that?"

Jeremy shrugged his shoulders. "I don't know."

"Do you think we ought to give him a bundle?"

"I guess so. He has the password."

Again came the high-pitched voice, very insistent this time.

"No Bohea for Boston!"

"We'll have to take a chance, Del. He knows the password."

A bundle was shot down the chute.

Everything had gone smoothly. There was only one bundle left.

"No Bohea for Boston," a voice called up the chute.

Down went the final bundle.

Then, just as Jeremy and Del were congratulating themselves on a job well and smoothly done, trouble broke out.

Queue decided to get into the fun.

As the last bundle hit the stable floor, Queue grabbed it and dashed out of the barn.

"Come back here. Stop! Drop that!" the voice below cried out.

Jeremy and Del leaped for the ladder, and scrambled down. The man had set off after Queue. Jeremy and Del were right behind. The man soon gave up the chase, but the children kept on.

If the bundle got into the wrong hands—the hands of a British soldier, perhaps—the whole plot might be discovered.

Queue was ready for fun. First he pranced close to Jeremy almost near enough to be caught. Zip, he was leaping toward Del, shaking the bundle with "try-and-get-it" glee.

But Queue's hatred of the British soldiers was his undoing. All of a sudden, he dropped the bundle. The hackles on his back rose. He uttered a low growl. He had sighted a Lobsterback approaching.

Jeremy dashed for the bundle Queue had
dropped. The British soldier reached it at the
same time, and grabbed the bundle.

"Here now, what's this? What's a-goin' on
here?"

Jeremy breathed a sigh of relief. It was Sergeant
Stubbs.

"It's nothing, Sergeant," Jeremy said. "Del and
I are just taking this bundle home."

"Home, you say. You're goin' the wrong way,
aren't you?"

"Please, Sergeant, give it to me," Del pleaded.

"Not till I've had a look at it."

The sergeant inspected the bundle. He
scratched his head, bewildered.

"Now who would be wantin' feathers and an
old blanket but an Indian? And some red paint
here, too. Goin' on the warpath, be ye?"

Stubbs unscrewed the bottle top, and took a
sniff.

"Hmmmm. Smells good."

Jeremy stepped forward. "It's just a costume.
For—for a pageant," he finished weakly.

Stubbs still looked suspicious. Jeremy had to admit to himself it was a pretty lame excuse. What would he be doing out here at this time of night with a costume? Stubbs relented, though, and handed the bundle over to Jeremy.

"Now get along home with you. Lieutenant Snipe is playing Indians, too. He's on the warpath tonight."

Sergeant Stubbs, chuckling at his own joke, marched off.

Jeremy and Del hurried home. Tomorrow was the big day.

CHAPTER THIRTEEN

Party Time

A COLD, windy drizzle swept Thursday, December 16, 1773, into history. The drizzle, intermingled with wet snow, fell from low-hanging clouds. As a good omen, however, wind blowing from the southwest gave promise of better weather later in the day.

Regardless of the weather, the town of Boston was rapidly filling up with people from surrounding towns. An air of excitement could be felt everywhere. True, a meeting had been called at Old South for that day, but the meeting alone wasn't responsible for the crowds which kept surging in. Wild rumors were circulating throughout the town that something more than just the meeting was going to take place that day.

Although not more than fifty or sixty people knew about the plans for the Tea Party, everyone sensed the coming of some big, important event.

Late in the morning, the excitement grew when Governor Hutchinson, alarmed at the growing crowds, left town for the safety of his country home in Milton.

By early afternoon, Old South was filled. A crowd of thousands milled about in the streets outside the meeting house. Over seven thousand Sons of Liberty were present.

A holiday spirit had taken over the town by the

time Jeremy and Del left their home and headed for Old South. Their mother's warning, "Please be careful, children," made them wonder if she knew what was going to happen that night.

It had stopped raining, and the heavy clouds went tumbling by overhead, leaving patches of clear blue in their wake. It was going to be a fine evening after all.

Jeremy and Del forced their way through the crowd. Jeremy wanted to be at the early part of the meeting. Later he would have to leave for Griffin's Wharf.

They entered the meeting house as cheers shook the building for the speech Sam Adams had just made. Next to speak was Josiah Quincy. Shouts of approval rang out as Quincy denounced the Government of England, the King, Governor Hutchinson, the East India Company, Parliament, and everyone else connected with the tea shipments.

Candles were lighted as the early winter night came quickly in. Jeremy pressed Del's hand.

"Stay right where you are, Del, so I can spot you quickly. I have to go now."

"Oh, Jeremy, take care of yourself," Del pleaded.

"I'll be all right, Sis."

Again he squeezed her hand, then made his way out through the excited throng.

It was quite dark out now. The moon was just peeking over the water of Boston Harbor. Only a few white clouds rolled along the sky.

Jeremy, just before going on Griffin's Wharf, threw off his greatcoat, folded it, and hid it in the shadows. He took a bottle from his pocket, and smeared its contents over his face and hands. Quickly he stuck feathers in a band he had brought, and tied it around his head. A long blanket covered his body.

No one paid any attention to the lone Indian

No one paid any attention to the lone Indian who took a position on the dock where he had a full view of the three tea ships.

Jeremy had been there only a short time when he heard the bell in Old South toll five times. Five o'clock. The sailors should soon be leaving their ships.

Jeremy waited. Time seemed to go by at a turtle's pace. Why weren't the seamen leaving their ships? Had news of the planned Tea Party leaked out?

Jeremy was growing panicky when he heard the clock bell toll the half-hour. Five-thirty. Still the seamen hadn't left the ships.

Back at Old South, Del was getting nervous, too. Every few minutes, Sam Adams would glance in her direction, waiting for her signal.

The crowd in Old South was getting restless. They had been listening to speeches for hours. Expecting action, the crowd now wanted it.

Del saw Mr. Adams approach Josiah Quincy, and whisper something. Quincy arose to speak again.

"I see the clouds which now rise thick and fast upon our horizon," he said. "The thunders roll and the lightnings play, and to the God who rides on the whirlwind and directs the storm I commit my country."

In the crowd outside, people murmured angrily at an Indian who was pushing, shoving, forcing his way to the entrance of the meeting house.

"Here now, you Indian, cease your pushing."

But Jeremy paid no attention to the remarks directed at him. The seamen of the tea ships had finally left their ships. Jeremy had raced at top speed to Old South. Now, gasping for breath, he reached the entrance.

He held up his hand, waving it violently to attract Del's attention. She saw him. Jeremy nodded his head, and Del passed the signal on to Mr. Adams.

Mr. Adams stepped up to Josiah Quincy, halting him in the middle of a sentence.

Then Samuel Adams, the patriot and leader, spoke the words which were to spark the first great act in the events leading to America's war with England for independence.

Adams held out his hand. Silence came over Old South Meeting House. Clearly, boldly, Adams spoke:

"This meeting can do nothing more to save the country."

This was the signal. Instantly war whoops shattered the silence which had followed Adams' words. The shouts fairly rattled the windows of the building.

Some fifty "Mohawks" suddenly leaped up in the rear of the building. Whooping, howling, brandishing hatchets, they formed a line and did a war dance out into the street.

The crowd quickly formed behind the file of "savages." A weird picture took shape in the brightening moonlight. In Indian file, the disguised patriots danced crazily through the streets on their way to Griffin's Wharf. Shouts rang out into the bright air. Dogs, Queue among them, raced along with the mob, barking wildly.

As the crowd, led by the "Indians," reached the entrance to the wharf, it halted. The British Guard, patrolling their posts, stopped in amazement at the sight. Believing they were to be attacked by a mob of maddened Indians, the guards tossed aside their muskets and took to their heels. A roar of laughter went up from the crowd as the Lobsterbacks fled up the street, Queue and some of the other dogs close behind them.

Quickly, now, the "Indians" moved onto the wharf. The group was divided into three parties, one for each ship. The "savages" swarmed up the gangplanks, crossed over the decks, and started opening up the hatches.

Jeremy was in the group which boarded the *Dartmouth*.

It took only minutes to tear off the hatches. Some of the "savages" disappeared below. Soon chests of tea were handed up from below with rhythmic efficiency.

If Captain Hall was on board, he wisely decided to stay in his cabin and not interfere. Any members of the crew still on board also remained in their quarters. There was no interference on the other ships, either.

Soon hatchets and "tomahawks" were smashing away at the tea chests. It had become quiet as the patriots went about their task of dumping the tea. Even at a distance, the sound of hatchets smashing chests could be heard.

Jeremy was having a hard time shoving one of the chests over toward the rail of the ship.

"Let me help you with that," he heard a quiet voice say.

Jeremy straightened up quickly and looked sharply at the "Indian" standing beside him. It couldn't be! It just couldn't! But it was!

"Father!" Jeremy cried out happily. "It's you."

"Yes, Jeremy."

"But—but—I don't understand."

Giles Winthrop smiled.

Understand or not, Jeremy was so happy, his heart was singing. Tears of joy welled up in his eyes. He stepped around the chest and threw his arms around his father's neck, burying his head in his father's broad shoulder.

"Come now, son. We're Indians with work to do."

Together they took chest after chest of tea to the side of the ship and sent its contents spilling into the waters of the harbor. It was Jeremy's boast, and a true one, that he and his father dumped more chests of tea than any other pair in the Tea Party.

In all, three hundred and forty-two chests of tea were dumped into the harbor that night, eighteen thousand pounds of tea. It was valued at nearly $100,000. It took three hours to do the job.

When the last chest of tea had been dumped, Jeremy and his father walked over to the dockside of the *Dartmouth*. They looked down, and there in the glare of torchlights, they saw Del and Mistress Winthrop. Giles Winthrop put his arm around Jeremy's shoulders, and father and son waved at the mother and the daughter standing on the wharf. Del was jumping up and down, waving back frantically and excitedly, as Mistress Winthrop tried to hold her back. But Del pulled loose, and dashed up the gangplank to meet her father and Jeremy. She almost bowled her father over as she threw her arms about him.

The family, all together, tired but happy, left the wharf and trudged slowly home.

Behind them the tides were carrying the tea out,

past Wing's Shipyard and the South Battery, past Gibbs's Wharf and Wind Mill Point. The next morning the shores of Dorchester were covered with Bohea. "No Bohea for Boston" indeed. But the spirit of independence had been brewed.

All had gone well. The Tea Party had been most orderly. Nobody had been hurt. No property was damaged—except the tea chests.

CHAPTER FOURTEEN

Family Reunion

THE Winthrop family was gathered in the living room of their home. They had just returned from the Tea Party, and were still laughing at Del's remark.

"Boston Harbor was a teapot tonight. Just a great big teapot," she had said.

"Giles," Mistress Winthrop said to her husband, "you look really terrifying. Do go wash that stain from your face, whatever it is. You, too, Jeremy."

"I could tell you what that stain is, Mother," Jeremy said, with a knowing look at Del.

"Don't you dare, Jeremy Winthrop!" his sister warned.

Jeremy laughed, and left the room with his father. They returned in a few minutes, and all sat down to talk about the Tea Party.

In the midst of the conversation, a high voice,

imitating that of a woman, pierced the room. "No Bohea for Boston!" it exclaimed.

"Father!" Del cried out excitedly. "It was you. *You* were the one with the funny voice last night. But how did you know the password?"

Father just looked wise.

"You must have known all along what we were doing," Jeremy said wonderingly.

Before Giles Winthrop could answer, a knock was heard on the front door. Jeremy opened it. Samuel Adams stood on the threshold.

"I apologize for intruding on this happy family," he said, on entering. "But could I borrow the services of Patriot Winthrop once more tonight?"

"Certainly, Sam," Giles Winthrop replied.

Del and Jeremy looked at one another, puzzled. Patriot Winthrop? Had their father, all this time, been working with Mr. Adams, when they had thought him to be on the other side?

"It will take only a few minutes, Mistress Winthrop," Mr. Adams assured her. "Paul Revere is waiting outside. He must ride to New York and Philadelphia with news of our Tea Party. I would like the assistance of Giles to help me draft the message."

"I'll brew us a cup of tea while you write the message," Mistress Winthrop replied.

"Bohea?" Mr. Adams asked, laughing.

"No. I'm afraid it will have to be catnip and pennyroyal."

Laughter followed Mr. Adams and Mr. Winthrop into the study. They returned just as Mistress Winthrop came back into the room with a pot of catnip tea.

"Jeremy, would you take this out to Mr. Revere?" Mr. Adams asked. "He is impatient to be off." He handed Jeremy the note. "You may read it if you like."

Del, on tiptoe, poked her head over Jeremy's shoulder to read the hastily written note:

Gentlemen: We inform you in great Haste that every chest of Tea on board the three Ships in this Town was destroyed without the least Injury to the Vessels or any other property. Our Enemies must acknowledge that these people have acted upon pure and upright Principle. . . .

When Jeremy came back into the house, there was a frown on his face.

"Father, could I ask you one question?" he said.

"Indeed, you may, Jeremy," his father said.

Jeremy hesitated. He was ashamed to ask the question, particularly since Mr. Adams was still there. But he gathered up his courage and spoke.

"The other night—night before last, I think— Del and I saw you going into Governor Hutchinson's mansion by the back door. Why did you go there?"

"May I answer that, Giles?" Sam Adams asked.

Mr. Winthrop nodded his head.

"Your father, Jeremy, went there at my request. We had to know what plans the Governor had for disposing of the tea. Your father, being on the board of governors of Harvard, had to work closely with Governor Hutchinson in college matters. Therefore, he was the ideal man to work with us and keep us informed on the Governor's plans."

Mr. Adams' remark made everything clear to Del and Jeremy about their father's actions.

"You'll learn, Jeremy and Del," Mr. Adams continued, "that in any great movement, such as the one we are now engaged in, there must be those who work in secret, behind the scenes. In many ways, it is much harder for them than for us who can speak and act openly in public."

Jeremy and Del went over to their father, put their arms around him, and pressed their faces against his.

"And now, children, I think it's time for bed," Mistress Winthrop said in a no-nonsense voice.

Jeremy and Del said good night to Mr. Adams and their parents. They went upstairs to their rooms, tired but happy. They had taken part in the planning, had issued the invitations—in the form of the Indian disguises—and had attended the greatest Tea Party history was ever to know.

Jeremy and Del went over to their father

Later, Samuel Adams' distinguished relative, John Adams, who became the second President of the United States, wrote in his diary these thoughts:

"There is a dignity, a majesty, a sublimity in this last effort of the patriots that I greatly admire. The people should never rise without doing something to be remembered. The destruction of the tea is so bold, so daring, so firm, intrepid and inflexible, and it must have so important consequences, and so lasting, that I cannot but consider it an epocha in history."

About the Author

ROBERT WEBB was born in Dayton, Ohio, but has lived near Boston in recent years. Inspired, perhaps, by his own Cape Cod forefathers, he has taken a deep interest in that state's early historical characters. He has been at various times a businessman, a newspaper reporter and editor, and a top-flight public relations expert. The author of several well-regarded adult novels, he now concentrates on writing for children and has, in his own youngsters, Kirk and Judy, an admiring though occasionally critical audience.

About the Artist

E. F. WARD, a native of White Plains, New York, is well known in both the book and magazine fields for his striking illustrations, several of which have won special awards. He has done intensive historical research, particularly on the Revolutionary period. Besides painting, his chief hobbies are sports and politics.

About the Historical Consultant

PROFESSOR LOUIS SNYDER was born in Maryland and attended St. John's College in Annapolis. Then he went to Germany for graduate study and took his doctorate at Universität Frankfurt am Main. For the last seventeen years he has taught at the College of the City of New York, where he is now Associate Professor of History. He has written many articles and reviews, and is editor of A TREASURY OF GREAT REPORTING.

OLD
NORTH
CHURCH